What had he seen . . . ?

He opened his mouth to speak, but confusion flickered across his face as his eyes caught hers. Cat's dark lashes lowered, veiling the depth of her emotions, but a slight tremor betrayed her and he took her in his arms.

Despite the day's humidity, when Raff pulled away Cat felt a sudden chill. His hands unclasped hers from around his neck and she yanked them back, hugging herself, steeling herself against the cold blue stare that slowly iced his face.

"Do you make it a habit of kissing strangers?"

The words of revulsion dealt her a swift blow, and, as she reeled from it, her mindless arm arced upward in desperate defense. Somehow she stumbled into her room, unattended, where she flung herself headlong across the bed. Feeling too luckless for death, Cat slowly realized that the throbbing in her arm was quite real.

One by one, she slipped her fingers out of their silken confinement, staring in disbelief at the purple swells that raged about each knuckle. She had not slapped Raff at all. Instead, her doubled fist had socked him squarely in the jaw!

HAND ME DOWN THE DAWN

Mary Harwell Sayler

Serenade/Saga
BOOKS
of the Zondervan Publishing House
Grand Rapids, Michigan

HAND ME DOWN THE DAWN
Copyright © 1985 by Mary Harwell Sayler

Serenade/Saga is an imprint of
The Zondervan Publishing House
1415 Lake Drive, S.E.
Grand Rapids, Michigan 49506

ISBN 0-310-46652-0

Edited by Anne Severance
Designed by Kim Koning

Printed in the United States of America

85 86 87 88 89 90 / 10 9 8 7 6 5 4 3 2 1

*To the protectors and lovers of Florida,
where plant life blooms, wild life abounds,
and bubbling springs flow free and pure.
Siloam Springs is a composite of these natural
wonders
which are given by God, enjoyed by all,
and protected by the caretakers of beauty-filled
tomorrows.*

CHAPTER 1

CAT CALDWELL TOSSED the broken shovel beside her father's grave and stomped the fresh mound of dirt with irreverent fury.

"Old man! Old man!" She wailed the only benediction beneath a canopy of scraggly pines.

At the moment her muscles ached more than her heart. She'd spent two days digging the rocky soil beside her mother's grave because she'd promised her father they'd be buried side by side.

"I should have buried you with her eight years ago!" she cried.

The heel of her boot packed the dirt hard. She hadn't been to church since she was nine—since Ma died—yet instinctively she fashioned a cross out of splintered boards and marked the raw mound. It didn't occur to her to pray or to sing a hymn, but the recurring thread of her song, unfinished and unbidden, wove through her thoughts.

Dark, oh dark, the sudden night has fallen.
Bleak, oh bleak, my heart is hanging bare.

7

The haunting melody snapped abruptly as Cat leaped to her feet and fled down the slope.

In the empty, bottle-strewn yard below, a sagging henhouse greeted her silently, a skeletal reminder of life past. Before Ma died, the well-kept house and yard sang with activity and Pa's lively tunes.

It had been Cat's job to gather eggs and, with sleek pigtails flying, she'd dropped them into her starched apron, cracking most of them in the process. Ma never scolded, but one day she'd said brightly, "Catherine, I'd make you a cake if I had enough eggs to spare." After that, Ma had plenty.

But there were no more cakes and no more songs after Ma died. Cat raised generations of squawking chickens and sold the eggs to buy sugar, flour, and other needed supplies. During the winter just ended, a succession of hard freezes had wiped out most of the stock. Now it was late March, 1895, and she'd killed the last hen three nights ago for soup. It hadn't done Pa much good.

The rotting porch creaked as she pounced through the door without bothering to wipe her muddy boots. She wasn't staying long enough for it to matter, and she'd given in to the dirt years ago anyway.

"That Caldwell girl is a sorry alley cat!" young Catherine had often heard on her rare visits to town. Despite the wrinkled noses, no one thought of giving her soap or teaching her how to make it, so the problem and the nickname stuck until Cat no longer cared. If anything, she'd come to like the image of herself as tough, independent, spirited.

She crept now through the dark room with its lingering odor of death. Her calloused hands were torn from the broken handle of the shovel, and the tight muscles on her thin body begged for sleep. For a moment the lumpy mattress tempted her, but Cat was determined to travel as far as she could before nightfall. If she were lucky, she'd make it to the railroad tracks before the train came. If not, she'd follow the rails to the next town.

Hastily Cat wrapped a wedge of dry cornbread in a grayed cloth and stuffed the pockets of her overalls with apples. She patted her throat to make sure that Ma's locket hung safely beneath Pa's flannel shirt, then she glanced around the room. There wasn't much else to take. She'd sold Ma's brooch and the good dishes some time ago, but there was the tin cup, dented and small, that she'd used since she was a child. She slipped it into Pa's jacket along with a box of matches and his knife.

She was grateful for the warm clothes, a scant inheritance from her father. Cat had outgrown her own clothes years ago, and now that Ma's dresses finally fit, they'd given out from early and frequent use.

Once Cat had tried to cut and stitch a printed cotton sack into a usable garment, but the sleeves had stopped her. She'd used the tunic for underwear, instead, smelling faintly of flour. When her appearance thoroughly disgraced the ladies of Piney Grove, a few well-meaning souls had ventured over with dainty slippers, discarded ribbons, and one serviceable green dress. They might have come again if Pa had not scared them off during one of his moaning prowls through the graveyard. But Cat had worn the green dress threadbare and stuffed the ribbons beneath her mattress ticking.

Remembering, she searched for a ribbon now. Mice had eaten through most of the treasures, but one—a black grosgrain—would do.

With a makeshift comb, Cat tugged at dark brown tangles and smoothed her long hair just enough to plait it. Impatient to be off, she wound the braid on top of her head and tied it tightly with ribbon. Then she yanked Pa's stocking cap over her ears and peered into a broken piece of mirror.

9

"I guess you'll pass for a boy," she told her solemn reflection. Hopefully the disguise would keep her safer on the long journey than the sight of a young girl traveling alone.

A final pat reassured her that the locket was still there. Then, without looking back, she slipped into the afternoon sunlight.

Overhead, the red flash of a cardinal caught Cat's eye, and she echoed his clear notes of "Pretty bird. Pretty bird." Momentarily fooled, he swooped closer, then was gone.

The question of where she herself was going didn't trouble Cat. The railroad tracks, recently standardized from state to state, now pushed southward into Florida, which beckoned mysteriously.

Florida. Feast of Flowers. Cat pictured the lushness and recalled the sweet taste of oranges that her teacher had once shared during those brief school years. Never had Cat tasted anything like it, and she imagined that the state abounded in citrus and fresh bubbling springs. Her teacher had displayed a yellowed newspaper clipping about a place called Siloam Springs, and Cat had rushed home to tell her mother about it.

"Just think! The water is so pure you can see clear to the bottom. People come from all over the world, Ma! Oh, let's go there! Please!" she begged.

"It does sound wondrous," Ma had agreed. "If I don't get there, you can see it for the both of us."

"Oh, I will, Ma. I will!"

But school was soon as remote as Florida. Cat tried to fill Ma's shoes, but the busyness and the shame over her own bare feet prevented her mingling with the town children in their store-bought clothes. She didn't know that the recent depression had left many youngsters as ragged as she, and by then it would not have mattered. Pa couldn't be left even for an hour without wandering off.

10

As his health declined, Cat thought about the Springs and the warm Florida sun. Thinking they'd be good for Pa, she'd questioned the station manager about train travel, but Pa had refused to leave his wife's grave. At least she'd tried. And, in the trying, Cat had found a sense of direction.

What she would do, how she would live when she arrived, was of little concern to her. She'd survived before, and she could survive again. But this time would be different, she thought. Life in Florida was better, was heaven. It just had to be.

CHAPTER 2

CAT HUDDLED IN THE CORNER of an empty cattle car, trying to ignite a scanty pile of dried chips. On the second attempt, she succeeded in starting a small but adequate blaze and, feeling warmed, she leaned back her head and slept.

When she awoke the fire had burned out, but daylight speared through ample slits in the walls. She'd had nothing to drink since she'd hopped on the south-bound train, but she'd finished the cornbread, sharing the last crumbs with her tiny traveling companion, a field mouse.

Greedily now, Cat bit into a juicy apple, devouring it and then another before her thirst and rumbling stomach were satisfied. Then she rolled the chewed cores in the direction of the mouse.

"Where are we?" she asked her companion.

Standing up, she stretched her aching muscles. A peek through the slits didn't tell her much, so, having loosened the tightness in her arms and legs, she promptly curled up again. When she awoke the next time, the mouse was gone and it was dark. She lit another fire, lessened her hoard of apples, and dozed until morning.

In the early sun a stately row of trees lifted up crowns of fans. Palm trees! Cat pressed her nose against the wood slats for a better look. Flat land chugged past. Sandy and grayish, it was dotted with shorter, squatty palms and clumps of wild grasses. Her heart thumped rapidly and, for a brief moment, she wished that someone could share her excitement.

"Oh, Ma! This must be Florida! I'm really going for the both of us."

Throughout the long, uncomfortable journey, the train had lurched to occasional stops, briefly rousing her. Each time, Cat had held her breath, wondering if she'd be discovered. But no one had come near the car. Now the train squealed and scraped against the slowing track, and abruptly, the door slid open. Cat shrank back.

"You! Boy! Whadda ya doin' here?" a gruff voice sounded through the glaring square of sun.

Cat stepped out of the shadows, chin high. "I'm going to Florida."

"Well, now, so you are!" The man laughed suddenly. In one swift motion, the stocky frame descended on her, grabbed her around the waist, and flung her off the train.

The wooden platform did not cushion the impact of her face and shoulder, and the tin cup pocketed against her ribs. Painfully Cat drew out the flattened cup, useless now, and hurled it at the man. He yelped and grabbed his forehead.

Before he could leap at her again, Cat scrambled to her feet and ran as fast as her father's boots could carry her. Down the platform, her long legs raced; down to the river's edge she fled without daring to look back.

Gasping, she sank into a heap. Her trembling

13

fingers felt for the locket still dangling around her slender neck. Satisfied that it was there, she wrapped her arms around herself and sat on the ground, rocking.

She had stopped shaking by the time she noticed a pair of rather large feet, planted near her knees. Her spine straightened rigidly, and defiantly she looked up, expecting to see the man. The man she saw, however, looked back with concern.

"You all right, boy?" he asked.

His were the bluest eyes she'd ever seen.

Shaking off her dazed stare, Cat jumped to her feet. Immediately she regretted the hasty movement. Her shoulder hurt, her face throbbed, and her ribs rebelled against inhaling and exhaling. She winced.

Long fingers reached out and feathered her cheek, but Cat recoiled.

"Don't be afraid. I'm not going to hurt you." The voice, which had seemed soft at first, softened even more.

"Didn't say you were," Cat retorted.

"No need to get sore—though I expect that bruise is," he said, unperturbed. "There's a bottle of witch hazel on my boat."

He turned and walked off, apparently expecting her to follow, and, having nowhere else to go, she did.

The jacket hanging nicely on those broad shoulders was store-bought, she noticed, and the shirt beneath was plain, but not homespun. A man of wealth, she speculated, then felt annoyed that she was meekly tagging behind. She quickened her pace, but the exertion reminded her of her ribs. Deliberately she slowed, averting her attention to the river.

Wide and placid, the water expanded the shoreline more than any of the rivers Cat had seen before. Train tracks railed against the docks, and everyone seemed in an enormous rush. Cattle lowed and calves bawled in mild protest as they were loaded for shipment up

14

north, and Cat wondered if they would occupy her temporary shelter.

A canoe rigged with sails glided across the river, and a tugboat sounded its horn. There were so many vessels, and so glamorous, Cat thought—especially the steamboats with their large paddle wheels churning the water.

Cat wondered which boat was his. When she saw, she was oddly disappointed.

"What kind of boat is this?" she demanded.

"A raft," he answered good-naturedly, then disappeared behind a crate. When he returned, he extended the witch hazel and a clean cloth. Cat snatched them out of his hand.

"I'll do it myself," she grumbled, and, on second thought, added, "thanks."

The blue eyes inspected her thoroughly. "What's your name?"

"Cat," she answered without meaning to.

"I never knew anyone named Cat," he said wryly, and she sensed he was making fun of her.

"Just don't go making any remarks!" she snapped.

"I wouldn't dare." He held out his hand, and she saw he was smiling. "My name is Raff. Raff Jordan."

Cat shook the warm, strong hand and grinned. "I never heard of anyone named Raff," she said and they both laughed.

"It's short for Raphael—my mother's idea," Raff explained. "You been in Jacksonville long?"

Jacksonville! So, she was in Florida!

"Long enough," she answered, giving her swollen cheek another pat of the witch hazel.

Raff frowned. "Where you headed?"

Cat hesitated. She wasn't sure she wanted anyone knowing about her, but the man—Raff—had been kind, and she still needed his help.

"Siloam Springs," she admitted at last.

15

The thick eyebrows rose. "Really? That's where I'm headed."

Now Cat frowned. She'd hoped that he might tell her in which direction to go. Or, if she were really lucky, he might even be going part-way himself. But it was too coincidental for this stranger to target her exact location. She squinted at him.

"That's convenient," she said.

To her surprise, Raff threw back his dark head and laughed outright. Swollen cheek even redder, she sprang to her feet.

"What's so funny, Mister?"

"You are. No, wait. I'm sorry." He grabbed the seat of her overalls and pulled her back before she reached the dock.

"Let go of me!"

"Huh, uh. You're not going anywhere yet." His voice was stern as he pointed toward a small crate and commanded her to sit.

"You're as skittish and distrustful as . . . as . . ."

"A cat," she finished for him.

She noted his smile with satisfaction. He looked young through that flash of even teeth, yet she guessed him to be at least thirty or close to it.

"Now," he said firmly, "do you suppose I'm a dealer in child slavery, about to kidnap you?"

Cat doubted it, but she shrugged, silent.

"Or," he continued, "a pirate who will seize your wealth and throw you overboard as soon as we're afloat?"

She suppressed a smile.

"If," he went on, "you could see what a sad-looking little waif you are, you'd realize that your suspicions are humorous!"

The smile died and tears threatened. Cat sprang from the crate and glared at Raff with hands fisted.

"I'm not a . . . a 'waif' or whatever you called me! I'm strong, and I need a ride to the Springs, and if

16

you'll give me one, I'll load this *sad-looking* little boat . . ."

"Raft. And it's loaded."

"Then I'll . . . I'll row it or steer it or whatever you do!" She flung out her hands, exasperated.

"I have an experienced helper—Wyatt Tate."

"Then I'll . . . I'll . . ." She clenched her teeth against tears, against the curiously soft expression on Raff's face.

"Can you cook?" he asked gently.

"Of course, I can cook!" she spat at him. "How do you think I eat?"

He didn't answer, but held out his hand again. "It's a deal then? You fix meals for Wyatt and me, and we'll get you to Siloam Springs before summer."

Cat's hand dropped, and so did her swollen jaw. "Before summer!"

The amused look was back. "I didn't realize you were in a hurry," he said. He pointed toward a platform not far from the one on which she'd been tossed. "The train is quicker. It'll get you there in no time."

But the thought of being pitched off again did not appeal to Cat, nor did she like the prospect of being jolted around with a bruised body and no witch hazel. Floating on the river, fed and reasonably safe, seemed the better choice.

She thrust her calloused hand into his larger one. "It's a deal."

When Raff's helper returned, the unlikely crew set off. Before they'd gone far, Cat's suspicions were again aroused.

"You're going the wrong way!" she accused.

The blue eyes danced. "How do you figure that?"

"Rivers flow south!" she smirked. "This one has a slow current, but we're going against it."

"So we are. But, it happens, dear la—dear lad, that the St. Johns River flows north."

17

"I don't believe it!"

For the first time, the dark brows knitted in annoyance. "Believe what you like! But this river is one of the few with a northern flow. That's why the mouth of it is in Jacksonville. And," he added irritably, "the river winds south, down through the state, so that almost anyone traveling it will pass by Siloam Springs. Years back, my family stopped there and liked it so well they stayed."

The intended apology stuck in Cat's unpracticed throat. "They still there? Your family, I mean."

"I'm not married, if that's what you're asking. And my parents and sister died in the yellow fever epidemic a few years ago."

This time Cat said, "Sorry," and meant it.

The navigation of the raft occupied the men, leaving Cat free to explore. The snug logs, which were lashed together with cord across and diagonally, supported the weight of a trunk, an assortment of iron pots, and various other gear. In the center of the raft, three large crates had been set in a "U" and covered with tarpaulin, making a lean-to of sorts.

Reasonably sure that the men were busy and the raft wouldn't sink, Cat scooted under the tarp. She comfortably rearranged the bedrolls she'd found in the lean-to, then set about doctoring her wounds.

The soothing lotion kept down the swelling nicely. However, it was difficult to lug the heavy pots ashore just before nightfall. When Raff attempted to help, Cat slapped aside his gesture.

The next morning, she awoke stiff and crept about gingerly as she prepared breakfast. She wasn't about to complain or ask for help, although she didn't really think that Raff would leave her behind if she failed to fulfill the first day's bargain. But when she attempted to carry the pot with her limber left hand, she found that a single arm wouldn't support the iron weight. The pot and Cat went tumbling.

In a heap, much as he'd first found her, Cat peered up cautiously as Raff stood over her. Lines in his face, which she hadn't noticed before, pinched out a scowl. But he stood silent, waiting.

"All right! I *do* need help!" Cat admitted with resentment.

Still Raff didn't move. "What's hurt besides your face?"

"My ribs and shoulders," she mumbled.

"Does anything need setting?"

"No!" she shouted. "I can take care of myself!"

Lightly, he helped her up and swung the heavy cauldron onto the raft. "You're one stubborn little creature!" he barked, then avoided her for the rest of the morning.

In the days that followed, the aches disappeared along with Cat's wariness. One minute, however, she felt certain that she hated Raff, and the next she wondered at her vulnerability when he treated her with kindness.

Her relationship with Wyatt Tate was less tumultuous, and, therefore, more pleasant. Cat found herself relaxing in his company.

"Why do you call yourself a Cracker?" she asked him one evening as they dangled feet and bamboo poles into the river.

"I dunno," the boy grinned. "Some say it's cuz we're a whip-crackin' people."

Cat couldn't imagine this boy, placid as the river, with a whip. Her laughter danced across the water.

Wyatt studied her, puzzled. "I don't mean no offense, but you shore do have a funny laugh for a boy. How old are you?"

Cat wasn't used to lying, but she saw no alternative. If Wyatt knew that she was almost eighteen, he'd really wonder.

"I'm, uh, fourteen," she said, slightly choking on the words. "But don't you go telling anyone!"

Funny, Cat thought, that she trusted him with her secrets, even her lies. Perhaps, she decided, it was because he, too, had had hard times. From their conversations, she'd learned that Wyatt lived with his widowed mother and a half-dozen brothers and sisters of assorted ages. And, as they talked, Cat began wishing that the boy's family had been her own.

"You'll have to meet John," Wyatt said. "He's the second oldest, and Ma counts on him for fresh game. That John, he kin hit a pheasant at two-hundred yards with his rifle. Calls that ol' gun 'Dead-Eye,' and you'd think it was his best friend. Reckon he's about yore age now."

Cat wanted to change the subject, but not entirely. "Tell me about your Ma," she coaxed.

"Not much Ma cain't do! Never did get no schoolin', but she reads her Bible. Knows it kivver to kivver." The freckles on the boy's cheeks clustered together. "When I was a youngun, Ma had me learnin' verses—a new un each week."

A vague recollection stirred, reminding Cat of sitting stiffly on a wooden seat with her own mother while a fist slammed the pulpit and a thundering voice echoed the words in a huge book. Involuntarily, she shivered.

"'I am the way, the truth, and the life, and no one comes to the Father but by me'," Wyatt quoted. "I always liked that verse special."

"Why?"

"'Cuz Jesus is the only way."

Cat scowled. "To heaven, sure! But the only way I know here is hard work, and we'd better be getting to it."

Life on the river demanded little of her, however,

20

and at first, Cat wished it would last forever. She'd spent years worrying about Pa, about chickens, about inadequate food and unending chores, and now her primary occupation was to rest and drink in the wonder of her lush green surroundings.

At night, the swooshing sounds and rocking motion of the raft lulled her when they anchored. And during the day, she delighted in new discoveries of plants and wildlife. Filled with curiosity and questions, her mind nimbly searched the aqua-blue sky, skipped gaily through ancient live oaks, and dipped into the sparkling river.

Although she wouldn't admit it, she wondered about Raff, too. What was his life like? Why was he traveling the river? Did he always treat strangers kindly? But the questions she allowed herself to ask him were of another sort.

"Why are those ragged gray shawls hanging from the trees?"

Raff chuckled at her apt description, but for once, Cat took no offense. "That's Spanish moss, an airborne plant. We use it to pack oranges for shipping."

"I thought Florida would be covered with orange orchards." By now, the apple orchards back home would be budding.

"Down here we call them groves," Raff corrected. "Unfortunately the heavy freeze this winter ruined the groves, so you won't be seeing oranges for a while." He hesitated, but Cat's look of disappointment encouraged him to continue. "I lost the grove I'd been experimenting on near Jacksonville. It froze down to the ground."

Cat shared his grim look.

"I guess it was time to be going home," Raff mumbled, half to himself.

"Why did you leave?" Cat asked, then quickly added, "Not that it's my business." She didn't mean to pry, especially since she didn't want him asking her questions.

A half-smile played on Raff's lips. "I was twenty-three and wanted to do things *my* way. Maybe you can understand that." A note of sarcasm crept in and lingered. "My family was not, shall we say, pleased with a stand I'd taken—a preservationist stand which opposed their own."

Cat's thin eyebrows curved at the word *preservationist*.

"It's an unpopular label people use to identify someone who doesn't believe in the abuse of life, whether it be land or water, animal or plant." Raff's voice hardened.

"The phosphate boom hadn't begun yet," Raff went on, "but my father guessed it was coming. So did I. From there, we differed. He wanted the industry to expand rapidly, so he invested in it heavily. And I wanted it kept under control so that untrained prospectors who didn't care about Florida would be kept from brutalizing the land. We had words, and I left," Raff ended regretfully.

Cat didn't notice his sigh. The word *phosphate* had kindled old memories for her, too. Reluctantly she recalled her father's rare spark of enthusiasm after Ma died.

"Phosphate, Catherine! It's white gold for the taking!" He'd pleaded with her until she'd given him money from the sale of Ma's brooch, but the white gold poured from a bottle purchased with Ma's memory.

The pain of the needless sacrifice struck Cat now, and her green eyes darkened. What did Raff know about doing without? About dreams, dead and bitter. Yet, from the sound of it, he'd deliberately walked away from a caring family. For what? A disagreement? Pride?

"Have you seen what prospectors do to the land, Cat?" he asked now as he gestured toward the shore.

She shook her stocking-capped head. "No. Is it as bad as what people do to one another?"

He looked as though she'd struck him, then turned away, poling the raft at a faster than normal pace.

It's none of my business, Cat scolded herself. Yet she felt angry—with Raff, with herself, with something, someone undefined.

Grabbing the extra pole, Cat attacked the water, and the strapped logs moved furiously forward.

When they anchored later, Raff and Wyatt disappeared into the woods as they did each evening. Cat cleaned the fish for supper, wondering, as she often did, where the men went and why they were gone so long. Yet she wasn't anxious for Raff's return. She hadn't spoken to him all afternoon, and she frowned when she saw him returning alone.

With no words between them, he came toward her, his arms loaded with lightwood, or "lightard" as Wyatt called it. Cat motioned to the spot she'd cleared, and when he dropped the bundle, she selected the smallest pieces for kindling.

The wood beneath the iron skillet burned brightly with its hoarded wealth of turpentine, oil, and resin. Still silent, Cat wiped her sticky hands on the thighs of Pa's overalls and rolled the fish in cornmeal before placing it in the heated pan. The grease sizzled.

A twig snapped. And, with a sigh of relief, Cat noted Wyatt's return. Tonight she'd counted heavily on his friendly chatter.

"It's might purty here! Not so bad as we figgered, Raff." Wyatt poured himself a cup of the scalding coffee and heaped his plate with fresh fish and fried cornmeal. "I reckon we're gettin' a fair idea of things, don' you?"

"I'd rather not discuss it now." Raff answered firmly. He finished the last bite of flaky fish, set down

23

his plate, and rose from the stump on which he'd been sitting. "I think I'll turn in early." Then addressing Cat, he added, "That was a fine supper."

Cat hadn't noticed any difference in this meal of which he'd eaten little. She supposed he was simply acknowledging her presence, but, unused to compliments, his remark embarrassed her. She poked at the lightwood glowing red until she heard his footsteps die away.

She wanted to ask Wyatt what he'd meant about getting a "fair idea of things," but instead she skirted the subject.

"Why did Raff take the river?"

"Guess he don't like trains," Wyatt evaded. "Hey! Did I ever tell you 'bout the time I hopped that old train to Jacksonville?"

Disappointed, Cat shook her head.

"Well, I wuz lookin' for Raff in that grove of his," the boy began, then proceeded to entertain Cat with a long, amusing tale.

Slowly, Cat relaxed by the fire, enjoying Wyatt's company and his yarns. She'd intended to draw him out, but somehow the conversation reversed itself, and she found herself confiding her recent adventures.

"At least you weren't thrown off a train on your ear!" she ended with a laugh. Wyatt chuckled too, then they both fell silent.

The boy stretched out his legs. "So you don't have no family?" he asked thoughtfully.

Cat shook her head. "But I like hearing about yours."

"I like tellin'!"

"Did you know Raff's family?" Cat asked suddenly.

The cheery face sobered. "Cain't say I did. But I reckon they had a fallin' out. Pore ol' Raff. He hadn't been gone long when they took sick. Come back fast

24

as he could, but it was too late. Pert near tore him up, Ma says.''

Cat leaned forward, rubbing her arms against the sudden chill.

''What did he do then?''

''Went back to experimentin' with them oranges. He left the homeplace in the hands of a tenant, and that worked out fine as long as the goin' was good. But the freeze drove him out, I reckon. That left the house empty, so Raff offered it to Ma. But she says she's right happy in the place Pa built. I 'spect she is.''

The offer of his house to the Tate family astonished Cat, and she expressed her surprise.

''Raff's like that.'' Wyatt yawned as he doused the fire. ''Says the Lord's given him a right good measure, so he don't mind sharin'.''

When Cat had gone to bed on the thick blanket, which padded the rough, rounded logs beneath her, she thought again about Raff's reasons for taking the river. Did it have anything to do with his nightly disappearances? And, if so, what? She didn't think the men were involved in anything dishonest, but if they were, she didn't know why she cared.

Staring at the stars glittering overhead, Cat wished she could touch their warmth radiating through the cool night air. She wished she could understand the feelings that churned like a paddle wheel inside her at thoughts of Raff.

Sometimes she considered him the kindest man she'd ever met, except perhaps for Wyatt, and he was certainly the most generous. But his senseless journey, his senseless stand against his family troubled her, and her heart ached, thinking him a fool.

CHAPTER 3

THE APRIL RAINS hoisted up the earth's green buds with showering cords. Unless the lashing ropes threatened to capsize the raft, the men poled steadily southward with their determined faces lowered under the limp brims of their palmetto hats. During the worst torrents, which Wyatt swore would be even more severe "come summer," Cat curled up in the relative snugness of the lean-to, daydreaming away the hours.

Sometimes she sang to herself songs pulled from her memory, lively tunes suited for a fiddle, or folksongs, or the soothing chorus of some long-forgotten hymn. But try as she might, she was unable to push away the mournful tune that haunted her— *Dark, oh dark, the sudden night has fallen. Bleak, oh bleak my hearts is hanging bare. Waiting for a glimpse of light, I'm* . . .

The melody showered her with sadness and, wanting to escape it, she slipped out of the lean-to and into the cooling rain.

"What was the song you were singing?" Raff asked as soon as he caught sight of her.

Cat shrugged. "Just a song." She hadn't meant for him to hear.

"Oh." He looked as though he wanted to say more, but he didn't. "You're getting soaked. There's no need for you to be out here."

"I can . . ." Biting her lips, Cat stopped herself before she said, "I can if I want to!"

She couldn't help but notice how thoughtful Raff had been since their misunderstanding, and she suspected that Wyatt had fed his sympathy by telling Raff the little he knew about Cat's orphaned state. Not wanting to discuss it with him, however, she avoided mention of her past—and his.

"I can use a bath," Cat said now, and Raff laughed.

The fact that she usually did need one troubled her little, though she'd wondered a time or two since she'd met Raff what it would be like to feel scrubbed clean. Well, that could wait. At present, the accustomed dirt suited her boyish appearance, and Cat was loathe to part with that familiar comfort. How she'd maintained her disguise this long mystified, yet pleased her. Adjusting to other people was complicated, she'd discovered, and, if it had not been for her ample time alone, she didn't think she would have managed nearly so well. But the relationship of a man and a woman was another problem altogether.

When the shower ceased, Cat stretched out on the raft, drying the soggy flannel on her back. Facing the water, she dozed, rousing now and then to watch pads of water hyacinth float idly past.

"What . . . ?"

Half-asleep, she couldn't be sure if the sun-jeweled water were playing tricks on her or not, but she thought a floating pad of greenery had suddenly disappeared. She opened her eyes wider, and, moments later, another hyacinth sank from sight!

27

"Something is down there!" she shouted to Raff.

"There's always something in the water!" he called back. "Fish, snakes, alligators. . . ."

"No! Something is down there *now!*" she insisted.

Obligingly, he leaned over for a closer look, but she was the first to see the strange creature again.

"It's a giant potato! And it's alive!" she cried.

Raff burst out laughing. "People usually mistake the poor creature for a mermaid, but I never heard of one called a potato!"

Cat put her hands on her hips and glared. "Well, you're so smart—what is it?"

"A manatee."

Raff knelt down to touch the calloused-looking gray skin before it submerged. The man-sized creature glided slowly through the water, surfacing every few minutes for air. Cat watched, fascinated.

"What did you call it?"

"A manatee," Raff repeated. "The river is warming, or you wouldn't see them. Manatee can't tolerate cold, so they winter in the Springs south of here."

"Siloam Springs?" Cat asked hopefully.

Raff nodded. "Siloam is one of their favorites. The water temperature stays the same year round, and there's plenty of vegetation for them to feed on."

"Are they fish?" Cat asked. She didn't think so, but her limited schooling had provided few categories from which to choose.

"Mammals—they bear live young," Raff tutored. "They're probably the gentlest animals on earth."

Overhead a more familiar creature swooped, and she exclaimed, "A cardinal!" Funny that that red flash should appear in these junglelike surroundings.

Touched by the warm spring sun, late this year in coming, the dense foliage shot out new green arms, replacing the frost-browned leaves and spikes and branches. Giant green hands clasped over the narrowing river, cuffed by the tattered shawls of Spanish moss and braceleted by hanging vine. The beautiful and sometimes eerie landscape fashioned itself after the tropics, foreign to Cat's memories of rocky hills and barren fields.

"Back home we see cardinals in the snow and . . ." Cat's voice trailed off. "Pretty bird, pretty bird," she mimicked its whistle, and, hearing, Wyatt was impressed.

"Sounds jest like a cardinal!" he said with admiration. "Kin you show me how?"

Glad for something to do, she obliged. A hilarious lesson followed, alternating Wyatt's flat notes with well-keyed sounds from Cat, so true, so clear, that feathered throats responded from the woods.

A mourning dove cooed and Wyatt suggested, "Try that!" which they did until erupting giggles made it impossible to continue.

Cat leaned back in the dappled sunlight, feeling deeply contented. It had been so long since she'd played, since she'd laughed until her sides hurt, and the silliness left her light-headed and light-hearted. She wished she could sing out gaily, but the men were in ear-shot, and her melodic voice might give away her boyish disguise. So she hummed, drowsily, dreamily.

From a low-hanging branch, a vine swung, brushing Cat's shoulder as the raft crept steadily beneath. But, in the open, the vine clung, coming to life as it slowly slid down the bibbed front of Cat's overalls before it wriggled across the logs.

Cat froze. The dry scaly skin hovered near her boots as one greenish-brown end lifted itself, its tongue flickering, tasting, testing the air. Her own body still, Cat gradually fingered one arm toward the extra pole, and when she'd latched around it, she swung the improvised club down hard, smashing the snake's head.

The heavy thud sickened her. Its dull sound and the

29

raft's sudden tipsiness alerted Raff, but instead of the concern or praise she'd expected, he turned toward her with a disapproval on his face.

"Why did you kill it?"

She felt like swinging the pole at him. "I suppose you'd rather it had killed *me!*" she accused loudly.

"Oh, sure," he shot back sarcastically. "I always take in strays and feed them to snakes!"

Raff swept the limply coiled body into the river's current. "It wasn't poisonous," he said with a bitter note.

"How was I supposed to know?" Cat defended herself. "It didn't have a painted sign!"

Raff's lips twitched. "Actually, it did. But you're right, Cat. You had no way of knowing. Sorry I yelled."

For some reason, his tenderness unnerved her more than the snake had, and to her dismay, she began trembling visibly. Raff dropped on his knees beside her and draped his arm around her flanneled shoulder.

"It's all right," he murmured, his low voice alarmingly near her ear. "You're not the first to kill out of fear, Cat, and you won't be the last."

But Cat scarcely heard. Someone had once held her close like this. Her mother, she imagined. But, no, it wasn't quite like this—this strange comfort that soothed, yet stimulated.

When she'd calmed down, Raff patted her shoulder. "Are you all right?" he asked.

Cat assured him that she was, and Raff took up his pole again. As he stroked the raft forward, he explained the variety of snakes she could expect to find in Florida. Cat listened to his instructions about which snakes were enemies and which were not. But the lessons she heard were far less intriguing than the one she had *felt*.

For the rest of the day, the corners of her green eyes scanned Raff's movements as she tried to find a

30

category for her unfamiliar emotions. Perhaps this was friendship. Or the closeness between two people who liked one another. But, no, she liked Wyatt equally well, sometimes better than Raff. Yet the thought of Wyatt's arm around her, while not repulsive, was just not the same.

To her relief, they stopped early that evening to air out their rain-dampened gear in hopes of avoiding the musty-smelling, freckled black mold that Wyatt had defined as mildew. Cat was grateful for activity, for something to occupy her thoughts besides Raff.

He approached her now, looking apologetic. "Would you mind handling the gear by yourself?"

Glad to be alone, to be busy, Cat didn't object, nor did she question him. She was used to his and Wyatt's mysterious disappearances, though still she wondered.

While the men were away, Cat combed out her tangled wad of hair and rebraided it before yanking Pa's cap back over her ears. With her bruises long healed and her muscles now accustomed to swinging the iron pots onto shore, she set up camp quickly and spread out their gear to dry.

She'd collected lightwood for the fire and was clearing a circle of brush when a rustle of leaves alerted her to the men's return. She hadn't expected them so soon. When she looked up, however, no one was in sight.

"Who's there?" she called.

Her hand readied a stout piece of the wood, and as she did so, she recalled Raff's earlier comment. "You're not the first to kill out of fear. . . ." With ambivalent feelings, her fingers loosened, then tightened their hold. No, not fear, but self-preservation, she told herself. Surely Raff wouldn't object to that!

Two frail figures stepped from the woods, and Cat dropped her weapon. With eyes too large for their small pallid faces, the children stared at Cat, and she stared back. Their bare toes curled in the pine needles beneath their feet, and their bare legs exposed a generous sprinkling of scars and scabs.

"Is that smallpox?" Cat asked, not wanting them any nearer until she'd established if they were contagious.

The older of the two, a girl, shook her head.

"Then what are those scabs?" Cat insisted.

"Chigger bites."

The small boy squirmed under Cat's close inspection, and, with his round eyes looking into hers, asked, "Are you a boy or a girl?"

Cat's eyebrows shot up, and she glanced around quickly to be sure that the men weren't nearby. "Why did you ask that?"

"Yore hair's mighty long."

Cat laughed, relieved. "You've been spying on me!"

"We didn't mean no harm," the girl said. "We's jest out lookin' fer bird eggs."

Cat smiled at the young voices, so like Wyatt's. "Did you find any? Bird eggs."

The little boy raked his grubby toes through the sand. "Naw. They done hatched." He sounded disappointed.

"Baby birds! Would you show me?" Cat asked, excited.

"Shore. But they ain't good fer nuthin'," the girl sadly informed her. "Too bony to eat."

It had never occurred to Cat that some diets were far less superior to the ones she'd known, and the thought jolted her. She gasped. But experience told her that these independent children would not welcome her pity.

"Tell you what," she offered in a forced tone of lightness. "You show me the baby birds, and I'll fix you some supper—all you can eat."

With shy grins, the children's unwashed heads

32

bobbed up and down. Then, leaving the camp unattended, Cat followed them into the woods.

The children's bare feet nimbly skirted spiky plants and palms and leaped over rotting logs. But Cat's left boot had raised a blister on her heel by the time they finally stopped. She'd had no idea that the treasure was hidden so deep within the woods.

"Up thar." The girl pointed, cautioning, "Don't tech them or their Ma won't feed 'em no more."

Balancing on tiptoe, Cat peeked in on four baby cardinals. With their black eye patches lidded tight, the apricot-colored babies snuggled together in the twigged nest.

"Oh, they're precious!" Cat whispered her delight.

She wished she could stroke the soft down, but she'd promised the children, and, besides, she didn't want the babies to be abandoned.

Through the darkening trees, the sunlight slanted lower and lower. Cat hadn't realized it was getting so late, and she welcomed her small guides as night settled on them.

"Won't your ma or pa be worrying about you?" she asked as they headed back to camp.

"Naw," the girl assured her. "They know we kin sleep most anywheres."

But Cat had not counted on Raff's concern at finding her gone. When they neared the camp, she glimpsed him, pacing near the fire now lit, his eyes also blazing.

He heard them coming, and on seeing her, his eyes widened and his lips circled their relief. Then, just as suddenly, his face fisted in anger.

"Where have you been?" he demanded.

Never had Cat seen him in such a stormy mood, but her own emotions whirled to meet his. Ever since Ma died, she'd been accountable to no one, and she didn't like Raff's placing himself in charge.

33

"I've never asked you where you've been!" she shouted back.

He flung out his arm, batting back her words. "That's different!" he yelled. "You're supposed to be tending camp! What about our bargain? What if someone had come and helped himself to the gear while you were gone!"

He was right, and she knew it, but still she fussed, "You don't have to yell!"

Heavily, his arms dropped, and so did his voice. "I didn't know where you were."

She'd intended to apologize, too, but the sudden silence alarmed her, and when she looked around, the children had fled into the night.

"Now look what you've done!" she shouted.

"I haven't done anything but worry about you!" His voice rose again.

"You did! You did!" she screeched.

She flew at him then, pounding his chest with her fists and sobbing. Tears that she had not shed for Pa, for herself, for her loneliness, now flooded out of control, and she felt powerless to stop the unbearably wrenching grief.

"Cat!" Raff shook her shoulders. "Cat!" he firmly called again. Then he slapped her face, hard.

Her sobs burst mid-air, then died. "You hit me!" She rubbed her cheek.

"You were hysterical," Raff said. "Sit down and tell me what's happened. I don't even know what this is about."

Shakily, Cat collapsed near the fire, feeling foolish.

"The children," she sniffed. "You scared them away with your yelling." That she had yelled too shamed her now, and her eyes flashed, expecting Raff to say so. He didn't.

"I'd promised them supper if they'd show me the cardinal babies," she said, meeting his puzzled stare. "They've probably never had a decent meal in their

34

lives! They're so frail. . . ." Her voice broke as the tears started again—for the children, for herself—but this time the flow bathed and healed her spirit.

When she'd quieted, Raff handed her a plate laden with food, and commanded her to eat. She obeyed, too tired to argue, and as the nourishment refreshed her, she realized that the food was quite good.

"You didn't need a cook!" she accused him. But seeing his pained expression, she looked away, silenced.

A "waif" he'd called her—a pathetic-looking creature, not unlike the two children who'd so gripped her heart.

When Wyatt returned, Raff left the two of them in camp. He hadn't said where he was going, but Cat knew he was searching for the children. He'd never find them, of course, in their own territory with its fallen logs and thick underbrush for hiding. Yet the search wasn't entirely futile. This act of caring touched Cat in a way that his personal concern had not.

Sitting by the fire with Wyatt asleep on the raft, Cat wondered about the children. Had they ever been well-fed? Had they ever known the embrace of loving arms? And, would she ever know that touch again— from Raff, from someone else?

Unbidden, the haunting song welled inside her, expressing what she could not yet admit.

Dark, oh dark, the sudden night has fallen.
Bleak, oh bleak, my heart is hanging bare.
Waiting for a glimpse of light, I'm crawlin'
through the blackest spaces, lonely hopeless places.
I'm waiting for love's dayspring to be there.

Fingering her locket, Cat closed her eyes. "Oh, Ma!" she cried into the darkness. Then, exhausted, she fell asleep by the fire.

CHAPTER 4

CAT WOKE UP with a start. "Boys don't cry!" she scolded herself.

A moment of panic assailed her before she shook her thoughts, sifting out the fears from facts. The truth was, she no longer had a reason to protect herself physically from Raff or Wyatt. Her disguise had already given her enough time to know that both men could be trusted not to take advantage of a young lady traveling alone without benefit of protector. They were her protectors! And her friends.

Still, she was loath to part with her disguise. Even if she'd wanted to, she had no other clothes to wear, although it would be nice to toss aside the heavy stocking cap. For a second, she imagined the delight of her long hair, flowing loose behind her, clean and fresh, in the river breeze, and the picture tempted. But that same sight might evoke some new response in either man, and Cat simply didn't want to risk it. She liked the relationships the way they were, easy and uncomplicated, and she needed time to understand her own heart.

Raff confused her so! One minute he was yelling at her, and the next he was traipsing off after two half-wild youngsters he didn't even know! She wondered if he'd slept at all, and when he appeared at breakfast, his haggard look told her he hadn't.

"About last night . . ." she began, but he waved aside her intended conversation.

"I did what I could," he said, pouring himself a cup of thick coffee.

"I know that!" she retorted, wondering at their ability to irritate one another so readily. Deliberately, she lowered her voice. "I was going to say that I don't usually cry like a . . . a girl!"

Raff's dark head jerked toward her, his eyes sparkling with amusement, but his lips remained thin-set. "I don't doubt that, Cat, but it's all right to cry, you know."

She shrugged. "Maybe so, but don't go thinking I'm a crybaby!"

"That's one thought I've honestly never had," he said, but his laughter reassured her more than his words. "I'd come nearer calling you a tough little bobcat," he teased, "or a stubborn mule, but never a crybaby," he added softly. "And Cat." He waited until she looked at him. "I'm sorry about the children."

"Me, too," she said, lowering her head. The warm mug hid her trembling chin, and she sipped her coffee slowly.

"It must be hard having to fend for yourself," he said, studying her. "Wyatt told me you've been on your own awhile."

"He had no right!"

The blue eyes narrowed. "Still don't trust me, huh?" He unfolded his long frame from the log on which he'd been sitting, then scraped the remains of his breakfast on his tin plate into the fire. "For your information, Wyatt didn't just tell me. I asked. I could be harboring a criminal," he mocked.

"Well, you're not!" she snapped, then dumped her own plate on the smoldering flames. Grabbing her thin shoulders, he faced her squarely, his clear eyes penetrating deep. "Look at me, Cat!" he commanded sharply. "No one has to tell me whether or not you're trustworthy. I'm a better judge of character than that. But I am interested in your well-being, and believe it or not, I care."

"Why?" she pushed his hands away. "Because you feel sorry for me? Well, I don't want your pity," she proclaimed without waiting for his answer. "I can take care of myself!"

"I know you can. And I don't feel sorry for you, so stop feeling sorry for yourself!" he hollered back. Suddenly he grinned. "You sure do get under my skin, little kitten." And with that strange remark, he left her, open-mouthed and confused, by the fire.

When Wyatt awoke, Cat warmed his breakfast, scarcely aware of his amiable chatter. Raff's early-morning comments tormented her, and she didn't know what to make of them. Had she been feeling sorry for herself? she wondered. If so, she'd have to stop. But other thoughts puzzled her more: why did Raff trust her and why did she find it so hard to trust him?

Or did she? His actions had strengthened her faith in him many times over, and despite their frequent arguments, she felt they got along well. So why was she wary? What did she fear? she asked herself, and knew. She was afraid of being hurt.

"That makes no sense!" she told herself, scowling.

"What don't?" Wyatt asked, and Cat jumped. She'd forgotten he was there.

"Oh, uh . . ." She glanced around frantically, searching for a subject to seize upon. "That boat!" she said, pointing upstream. "Hasn't it passed us before?" If it had, she'd paid it no attention.

But Wyatt answered, "Reckon it might'uv. 'Spect

it's travelin' faster'n us. Could'uv gone where it's a-goin' and come back by now.''

"Even the alligators are faster," she returned disinterestedly.

Wyatt chuckled. "Raff ain't in no hurry. If he were, we'd be on the river instead'uv setting here, and he wouldn't be roaming the river looking for skint land.''

For the first time all morning, Wyatt's remarks cut through her thoughts, and Cat asked, "Is that what he does?''

Wyatt's cheery face reddened. "I reckon I got a big mouth.''

"Don't be silly," Cat snapped. "There's no reason not to tell me unless he's up to something deceitful.''

"He ain't! I swear!''

"Then tell me," she commanded.

"It's them prospectors." Wyatt spat into the fire. "Most of 'em come through here itchin' for white gold, and they don't even know what phosphate looks like. They're on the river, on the road, and on the rail, carryin' a heap o' tools that'd best be used for plowin' up a field.''

"And?" Cat encouraged him to go on.

"And they've done tore up the land!''

"But what can Raff do about that?" Cat asked, alarmed. She'd never been afraid for the men until now, and she shuddered at the thought of Raff's meeting with a prospector's pickax. "He doesn't plan on stopping anyone, does he?'

Wyatt shrugged, which did little to ease Cat's mind. "Hain't run into no prospectors. Most of 'em's done gone. Naw, Raff's jest scoutin' the land, tryin' to see how bad it's hurt.''

"Then what?''

"Then I reckon he'll study on what to do ter fix it.''

"He can do that?''

Wyatt grinned. "Raff kin do most anything he sets his mind to.''

But, Cat thought, Raff couldn't stop the yellow

39

fever that swept his family away any more than she'd been able to help Pa. Nor could he warm the freeze that iced his groves. Suddenly she ached with him— for his conflict with his family, his conflict with the times—and she wished she hadn't been so hard on him. No wonder he hadn't confided in her.

Apparently Wyatt sensed her sympathy, and he soundly thumped her back.

"Ever'body don't understand," he said approvingly.

Cat's eyes watered from the friendly whack. "About preservationists?" she asked, remembering the word Raff had used to describe himself.

Wyatt nodded. "Some folks'd call Raff a fool."

"Well, he's not!" she defended hotly. Furious that she'd once thought that herself, she attacked the tin plates and iron pot, scouring them until they shone.

Scrubbing away her anger, Cat remembered the cardinal babies and how careful she'd been not to disturb their nest. Perhaps she, too, was a preservationist, she realized. But instead of annoying her further, the thought had a calming effect. She and Raff were not as unlike as she'd feared. Not that it mattered, she told herself, but knowing quite well that it did.

The better part of the morning passed swiftly with odd jobs about the camp, and Cat gave no thought to the hour. The men often tramped the junglelike woods after dawn, especially if night or a storm came early the day before. But as the late April sun reached its zenith, Cat paced the camp, restless.

"Where is he?" she asked Wyatt for the third time.

Sprawling on the black sand with a pin oak for a backrest, Wyatt whittled a piece of hardwood, unperturbed. "Reckon he'll be here when he gets here," the boy ventured lazily.

Impatient, Cat stomped her foot. "Why is he taking so long?"

Wyatt arched his back, stretching. "I dunno," he yawned.

"Well, what *do* you know?" she asked with such vehemence that Wyatt grabbed his sides, laughing.

"You shore are fidgety," he chuckled. "'Minds me of my little sister, Sara Ann."

With a concentrated effort, Cat unruffled her exterior. "Do you suppose we should go looking for him?" she serenely asked.

"Naw. Raff kin take keer of hisself."

Wishing she had Wyatt's confidence, Cat reminded herself of the long knife Raff kept strapped to his side. She'd only seen him use it to clear a path through matted vines, but no doubt the sharp blade could wield a strong defense. His muscles, too, could thwart most enemies, Cat realized as she remembered with pleasure the firm outline of well-developed chest and arms beneath his cotton shirt. Yet, despite his strength and flares of temper, Raff Jordan was a gentle man, and something or someone's spoiling for a fight could catch him unaware.

By midafternoon, Cat could no longer stop her pacing. She'd imagined a dozen bloody scenes with picks and prospectors and a few more with ten-foot alligators of incredible tooth and jaw. It didn't help that Wyatt, too, was restless, having gathered enough lightwood and kindling to last for days.

"Haven't you seen any signs of him?" she asked as another bundle dropped onto the enormous woodpile.

"Nope."

"What if a coral snake bit him?"

"Then I reckon he'd die! But there ain't much chance of that," Wyatt added hastily.

"Why not?"

"'Cuz them snakes have sech a tiny mouth, you'd plumb near hafta stick in a finger or a toe to git bit."

"At least that presents no danger," Cat remarked dryly. "Wyatt, why didn't you go with him today?"

"He left 'fore I wuz up," the boy reminded her.

41

"True, but he usually waits," Cat mused aloud. "I wonder why he didn't today."

Without answering, Wyatt reddened, and Cat's suspicions mounted.

"Wyatt Tate! Did Raff ask you to stay in camp today?"

"Well, uh . . . that is . . ."

"He did! And you've been sitting around all day babytending me when Raff could be lying out there, wounded, or . . . or dead!"

"Aw, he's fine." But this time the boy didn't sound so sure.

"You get away from that woodpile and get out there right now and find him!" Cat ordered. "And don't you come back until you do."

"Yes, ma'am! I mean . . ." Wyatt halted and gave Cat a hard stare. "You sound jest like Ma when one of the younguns's run off."

"Your Ma's not a wildcat like I'll be if you don't find Raff!" But only hours earlier Raff had called her a little kitten. Cat shook aside the puzzling endearment and concentrated on the search. "Better take a stick of lightwood in case you need a torch. It'll be dark soon. And some water, Wyatt. He might be hurt. And . . ."

"Now see thar, Cat. I told you he'd be fine," Wyatt interrupted, pointing. "But shore looks like that wild boar ain't in too good a shape."

"The what?"

"That thar's a wild pig he's a-carryin'. Hmmm—Mmm. Looks like barbeque tonight." Wyatt dropped the lightwood and bounded toward Raff like a hungry puppy.

With the dead pig slung over his shoulders, Raff sauntered into the clearing and deposited the horned-snout carcass at Cat's feet. "I brought you a pair of shoes," he said as though he'd strolled to the store and back.

"You did what?" Cat shrieked.

42

"You need some shoes." Raff spoke in the patient voice of a schoolmaster. "Those boots are too cumbersome for you. And I thought you and Wyatt might be as tired of fish and corn mush as I am."

"Where have you been?" she demanded.

"You're welcome," Raff teased. "Come on, Cat. Don't tell me you've been worried about me?"

"He shore was!" Wyatt answered when she refused to do more than glare. "He plumb worried the grass to death, pacin'."

Cat supposed she should be grateful that Wyatt was referring to her again as "he" rather than "ma'am", but at the moment she was too angry to care.

"Don't you ever go off like that again without telling me where you are or how long you'll be!"

"Oh, I see." Raff's dark eyebrows arched. "You might do the same yourself."

"So, you're just trying to get even! Well, you made your point, and it's not funny, and you can stop smirking at me!"

Raff sucked in the corners of his mouth. "I wasn't smirking; I was smiling. But I didn't mean to worry you, Cat. Honest." Then turning to Wyatt, "I found a wild grove. If you don't mind putting in a few days' work, we can prune enough to save it."

"Shore thing."

"And what am I supposed to do while you two are saving oranges and killing pigs?" Cat asked indignantly.

"We're not going to kill any more pigs," Raff assured her, "unless your stomach and your feet are bigger than I think. But you'll be busy."

"Doing what?"

"Making your moccasins, of course."

Raff's words, however, proved not altogether true, and Cat found even more leisure time on shore than she'd had on the river. All but the largest iron pot shone from constant scrubbing, and that one escaped only because it was in use.

After skinning the small boar and fleshing its hide, Raff instructed Cat on the leather-curing method he'd borrowed from an Indian acquaintance. First she had to strip the bark from a storm-felled oak and boil it in the big pot until it yielded tannic acid. That was the hard part. The rest of the chore meant an occasional stir of the soaking hide, and after an idle day or two of that, she vowed it could rot and Raff with it!

With Wyatt gone, too, the hours passed slowly, and threads of her song threatened to entangle. She wished she could catch another glimpse of the Cracker children, but they alluded her, and even the alligator on the opposite low bank of the river offered no more entertainment than a branchless log.

Once, when a steamboat wheeled its paddles down the river, she nodded soberly as the tourists gaily waved. But then they disappeared as she'd known they would.

"You are feeling sorry for yourself," she scolded, annoyed that Raff was right. But doing something about it was difficult when she felt so trapped, so lonely. And that's when she heard the song.

The lively notes of a banjo skipped through the corridor of trees along the river. Cat realized the music from the steamboat had been falling on deaf ears, as far as she was concerned. But now she heard, and hearing, she smiled for the first time in days. There were songs all around.

A mockingbird warbled its canticle while a blue jay cawed, and Cat echoed a refrain. All the songs she'd kept locked inside burst out, and when they'd flown on familiar, long-forgotten wings, new tunes, new lyrics, flowed joyously until she ached for a pen and paper to write them down.

She did her best to remember, however, repeating the songs until they'd saturated her memory and her spirit. And the trees and the river and the sleeping 'gator listened until her throat tired and the tanning hide needed a stir.

She felt happy.

"I think that pig skin has soaked long enough," Raff commented the first week in May. "You look rested, Cat. Real good, in fact, so I hope you're ready for some arm-tiring work."

"What do I have to do?"

"Rinse the hide in the river tomorrow," Raff said. "Then you'll need to pound it and twist it until the skin is soft and pliable. Of course," he added gravely, but the blue eyes twinkled, "if your arms tire too much, you can chew the hide awhile."

Cat shot him a disgusted look. "Chew it yourself," she said before huffing off.

The next day, however, she was tempted when her muscles throbbed from pounding. But instead of gnawing leather, she went fishing with the long bamboo pole Wyatt had cut from a clump of tall shoots that grew from a low bank on the water's edge. Two bony bream, a catfish, and a fat trout rewarded her efforts, and she lay on the grass, eyes closed, lazily humming.

"That's a catchy tune," Raff said, sneaking up behind her. "Did it catch you a fish?" He chuckled at his own joke.

Startled, Cat sat up abruptly, and her bare feet, which had been dangling in the water, splashed forcefully, wetting down her overalls.

"Very funny," she said, glaring up at him.

"You'd laugh less if that water moccasin had taken a liking to your toes." Raff pointed to the brown-scaled creature gliding down the bank. "Best keep your eyes open or your boots on."

With a shudder, Cat scrambled up the grassy slope while Raff trailed behind, laughing softly. But when she stomped across the clearing to fetch her boots, he stopped her.

"Let's measure your feet."

"I can do it myself!"

"Oh? You've made moccasins before?" Raff taunted.

"I didn't say that!"

"Then we'll measure your feet," he insisted firmly.

She knew she needed his help, but the thought of his warm gentle hands on her feet and her ankles, sent tiny shivers rippling throughout her slender body. And so she sat stonily on a log, pretending she were elsewhere, while his knife traced the outline of each foot on the leather's underside.

Raff finished with a feathery tickle on her arch, and she jerked her foot out of his hand.

"You're awake!" he teased.

"Are you done?" she asked, annoyed.

He nodded. "But you'll need some fat."

She bolted from the log and rested small fists on either hip. "My feet aren't bony!"

Raff tossed back his head, laughing. "Oh, Cat, what am I going to do with you? The leather needs fat—lots of it—rubbed in well to make it softer."

"Then why didn't you say so!"

"I just did," he chuckled.

Snatching up the tanned hide, Cat stormed off to finish softening and waterproofing the leather, and each step marched to the tune of "why." Why did he make her so angry so often? Why did she feel helpless and vulnerable with him around? Why did she wish he'd go away? Why did she feel miserable when he did? Why, why, why?

"Hey, Cat!" Raff called out merrily. "Don't forget your boots!" And his playful laughter goaded her to growl.

CHAPTER 5

RAFF'S LIGHTHEARTED MOOD lasted until the steamboat came, and Cat felt herself relaxing in his amiable banter. He felt pleased, she knew, with the progress he and Wyatt had made on the wild grove, and he seemed to enjoy her questionings.

"How did the oranges get here?" she asked when Raff said they weren't native to the state.

"The Spaniards seeded Florida centuries ago, so every now and then you'll see an unplanted grove."

"Folks around here shore miss them oranges," Wyatt cut in as the three of them relaxed around the fire.

The boy chattered on, but Cat scarcely heard. Until then, she'd assumed that Raff's own attitudes about the land had motivated him to several days of hard labor, pruning and clearing the frost-eaten branches. But now it occurred to her that the Cracker children, whom she'd not seen again, would be grateful for the countless juicy meals restored to them. The thought touched her, springing tears, and to hide her watery green eyes, she batted the air, swatting at imaginary gnats.

With the warming weather, mosquitoes did indeed abound, and Cat rubbed witch hazel on the welts. Fortunately her thick overalls protected most of her, and she kept her sleeves pulled down. But when the threesome once again rafted the river, the pesky flies increased, discovering the most unlikely spots on which to feast.

"These mosquitoes are eating me alive!" Cat yelped. Her short nails clawed at the welts she could decently reach, and Raff's suggestion of turning her thoughts elsewhere was only slightly less irritating.

"They're worse on the river," Raff admitted when she complained again, "But don't worry, Cat. It won't be long, and you'll be more comfortable."

She stopped scratching. "What do you mean?"

"We're only ten miles or so from Siloam Springs."

"But . . . but you said we wouldn't arrive until summer."

Raff's dark head shook. "I said I'd get you there before summer," he reminded her. "And it is."

"But it's barely May!" Her protest sparked his obvious concern, but she couldn't disguise the seizing panic. She'd known this moment was coming, but not yet! Oh, why had she let herself relax? Why had she snuggled into the protective comfort of knowing Raff was nearby? For an instant, she hated him, hated her attachment to him, and then she knew. This parting was what she'd most feared.

She'd hardly noticed when Raff set down his pole, leaving Wyatt to guide the raft alone. But suddenly he crouched beside her, lightly draping his arm across her shoulder.

"Cat, I wish I could ask you to come with Wyatt and me to the homeplace, but I can't. Not now. We both have too much to resolve, and . . . ." Whatever he'd had on his mind went no further.

Abruptly Raff stood up, slapping a thigh with false heartiness. "You know us, Cat! Wyatt and I will probably top-work the trees on my land until we drop! Did I tell you how we do that?" he asked. When she remained wooden, he went on.

"After we've pruned the trees, we'll graft new stock onto the old root system. Since the grove is well-established, that will produce fruit quicker than planting new trees—although I expect we'll plant some, too. I'm thinking about top-working with that new strain of citrus Lou Gim Gong produced. I told you about him, didn't I?"

Cat nodded. She'd heard Raff's enthusiastic account of the brilliant horticulturist who'd immigrated from China, and she'd been interested. But not now. Not when her future was Spanish moss without a tree!

Well, her life was her problem, not his, and she'd not have him accusing her again of self-pity. Drawing a deep breath, she straightened her shoulders and tilted her chin high.

"Your groves may need you, Raff, but I don't."

"That's right," he answered, but his smile vanished and his jawline hardened. "You can take care of yourself—you've said so often enough! But listen, little wildcat. Don't let those claws get too sharp for people." And with that warning, he resumed his position, poling the raft.

Hands trembling, Cat snatched up the pieces of cut leather that had tumbled from her lap. She'd been in no rush to lace her moccasins with the strip of hide Raff had spiral-cut from a circle of the leather. But now she concentrated on lacing together the back-piece and vamp to the sole, weaving the leather thong in and out of the holes Raff had punched with his knife.

Her bare feet stretched before her on the raft, released from their clumsy prison of Pa's boots. Cat knew the moccasins would serve her comfortably and well. She just hadn't expected to need them so soon.

How long would it be? she wondered. How long before this makeshift home docked forever? Throughout the journey, they'd averaged a mere two miles a day since they traveled against the current and lingered on the land. But this close to Siloam, Raff might be inclined to hurry, and the five-day trip could take four days, or three, or two.

Then what? Where would she go? What would she do? Not having seen the Springs, it was impossible to know what awaited her, what choices she could make. And maybe she wouldn't even want to stay.

There were other towns, of course, and some they'd occasionally passed on the river. She'd look for work, something that interested her, something she could do. If that failed, she'd track down one of the empty Cracker cabins she'd spotted in the woods from time to time. With fish and berries and edible wild plants, she'd fare far better than she had before.

Having reminded herself of the options and her own abilities, the panic fled, but not the disappointment. What she wanted most Raff had denied. *Dark, oh dark, the sudden night has fallen. Bleak, oh bleak. . . .*

"No!" She wouldn't allow it!

"Did you call me?" Raff asked, but she shook her head and forced herself to hum a lively tune.

By early afternoon, storm clouds threatened, and Raff hollered to Wyatt that they'd make camp. The men had intended to maneuver around the *Starlight*, a steamboat loaded with cargo and more tourists now that the weather had warmed. But Cat pleaded with Raff to camp closer by.

"Couldn't we, please, Raff? I've never been on a steamboat before, and you could talk them into letting us come aboard. Please?" she asked with such appeal that Raff couldn't turn her down.

"All right," he agreed, responding to her rare smile. "If I don't take you, I've no doubt you'd go without me."

"He shore would," Wyatt added, "only he'd be tossed on his ear ag'in like when he snuck on that ol' train!"

Too late, Cat shot the boy a look to shut him up, but Raff didn't scold or comment. He merely stared at her with weary sadness etched upon his face.

"Why is the boat stopped here?" Cat asked, in hopes of distracting Raff's thoughts. "There's nothing around."

"Lightard." Wyatt intercepted her question. "Them river people make a right good livin' sellin' wood to them boats."

"Is that why we've seen so many small piers away from town?"

"That's what sum of 'em's for, yep," the boy said.

Delighted Cat realized she had another possibility for earning her living.

As the men tied the raft to a cypress piling, lightning flickered through the trees and, in the distance, thunder rumbled.

"Get what you need and hurry," Raff ordered. "I don't want you near the water or the woods when that storm hits."

"No problem. I'll hang in the air," she said, but Raff wasn't amused.

"I mean it, Cat. Scoot!" He punctuated his remark with a quick smack on the seat of her baggy pants.

His scowl forbade her arguing, and the gray-green eeriness of the sky persuaded her to hurry. Never had she seen anything like it. Even the birds were stilled.

Grabbing what they could, the three of them leaped onto the shore with Raff at the rear. He hustled them into a small clearing, and, as soon as he'd dropped the load he carried, he turned back toward the river.

51

Cat's moccasins touched his heels. "If you're going back, so am I," she announced.

"Don't be obstinate, Cat. I don't want your help!"

"That's too bad!"

Arguing, they broke into a run, leaving Wyatt to cover the supplies as best he could.

Since they'd never unloaded the raft completely in previous storms, it hadn't occurred to Cat that they'd do so now. But as soon as she saw Raff struggling with the heavy crates, she regretted her impulse to follow him. Wyatt's strong arms would have been of more use than hers. Undaunted, however, she hopped onto the raft and lugged what she could to shore.

An arrow of lightning speared through the tortured sky, and within seconds the booming thunder deafened their ears. Raff dropped a small crate on the riverbank, then scooped Cat into his arms and flung her over his shoulders.

"Put me down!" she yelled, thumping Raff's back with her fists, before the crashing storm silenced her.

Huge drops of rain splattered about them as they rejoined Wyatt in the clearing, and the three of them huddled together under a tarp as the thunder and lightning simultaneously split the overhead sky. Far off, a train whooshed by, and Cat expressed her surprise that the rails were so close to the river.

"They're not," Raff said grimly. "That sound means a tornado hit nearby."

The wind and Wyatt's quivering rustled the tarp. "I di'n't feel no thud. Must've hit 'crost the river."

"Yes, thank God," Raff answered. "Looks like we've been spared." His hold on Cat tightened as though he half-expected her to spring out into the storm. But instead she snuggled against him, content to feel his arm around her under the darkening canvas.

As soon as the sky's brief fury subsided, Raff threw back the tarp.

"It's passed," he assured them.

Regretting the loss of Raff's protective arm, Cat hopped up, hugging herself against the sudden chill.

"Good grief! What a mess!" she exclaimed as she saw the fallen limbs strewn around her. How had she escaped so many storm-thrown branches? Then, seeing one against the tarp, she knew. Raff had shielded her.

She'd assumed his arms meant comfort or caution, never guessing that he'd sustained a blow. Racing to catch up with him, she asked if he were hurt.

"It's nothing a warm soak in a tub wouldn't cure," he assured her with a half-smile. "But our cargo didn't fare as well."

When Cat saw the damage, she gasped. Miraculously, the raft hadn't flipped, but one large crate, which had been left floating, had split, spilling its contents, and a few smaller boxes bobbed downstream.

"Oh, Raff! I'm sorry! If I'd stayed put and let Wyatt help you, this wouldn't have happened."

His hand cupped her chin. "You meant well, kitten, and what's done is done. Some of it would have been lost anyway, but they're only things. What matters more is people."

Did he mean that? No! She jerked away. Maybe he did value objects less than human beings, but what about the trees, the land? Did that mean more? He'd left his family, hadn't he? And soon he would abandon her for the same reasons.

"What is it, Cat?" he asked gently. His blue eyes penetrated hers, questioning, but she turned away, knowing that nothing she could say would make a difference.

"Tell me what to do," she insisted without looking at him. "Maybe we can save a box or two."

Using a forked branch, Cat did manage, with Wyatt's help, to pull ashore a small box. The remainder gurgled and sank, resting somewhere on

53

the river bottom with Pa's boots. It was silly to let a loss like that bother her, she told herself, especially when Raff had lost far more. But it bothered her just the same, and she pressed Ma's locket against her for comfort. That and Pa's clothes were all she had left.

"Didya see that steamboat, Cat?" Wyatt asked, splashing up the bank. "Reckon it ain't got a scratch on it."

Until then, she'd forgotten about the glamorous paddleboat, but it could wait. Wet to their skin, the men shivered in the rain-cooled air before Raff insisted they stop their search.

Hurrying ahead to the clearing, Cat built a fire and set on coffee to perk. Then she piled fallen limbs, in one direction and another, until she'd built a ventilated mound for drying clothes and cargo.

When he reached the camp, Raff nodded his approval.

"Thanks, Cat. Would you help me out of these wet clothes?"

Horrified, she mutely pulled off one soggy boot, then the other, and turned them upside down by the fire. Meanwhile, Raff peeled off his waterlogged shirt and tossed it to her.

"Wait!" she hollered as he began to unfasten his pants. Quickly she flung the shirt over the drying mound. "That's a bad bruise on your back. Sit down while I get the witch hazel."

"The fish have it," he said wryly.

"Then . . . then . . . sit down anyway!" she commanded while she thought.

Raff sat, grinning at her discomfort. "What's the matter, Cat? Aren't you used to naked men?"

"I can't say that I am!" she retorted. Not knowing what to do next, she racked her brain until she realized what she'd been searching her memory for—Ma's loving hands rubbing away a bruise, a hurt.

Tentatively, her clammy palms touched his muscled back and instantly recoiled. He flinched.

"What are you doing?"

"I'm rubbing that knot on your back," she said. "Now be still!"

She wiped her hands on the sides of her overalls and tried again. Somehow her palms stayed put this time, and slowly, carefully, she kneaded the lump, circling the area with the heels of her hands. While she massaged, she bit her lower lip, remembering. Ma's tender treatment had always included a feathery kiss.

"That's better, Cat. Thanks."

"I'm not done!"

Swaying, Raff stood up. "Well, I am. And I'm getting out of these wet trousers."

"Suit yourself! I'm going fishing." Stumbling in her haste to get away, she almost forgot the bamboo pole, but, red-faced, she escaped, Raff's laughter echoing at her heels. What a sissy he and Wyatt must think her, but that was too bad!

Storm debris cluttered the water's edge, snagging Cat's line, and she yanked the pole impatiently.

"Can't see a thing!" she muttered to herself. The rain had stirred the river bottom, muddying the water.

Dutifully, however, she caught a large trout and a mullet for supper before laying down her pole. Then, with knees drawn up under her chin, she stared dreamily down the river.

What a strange sensation it'd been to touch Raff's back! Hazily she remembered a hot summer day when Pa had stripped to the waist, working in the cornfield, and when he'd come in, Ma had lemonade waiting. But, no, that wasn't the same. Not for her.

Was it for Ma? Did she like to rub Pa's back, feeling the hard muscles under the soft flesh? Did she long to be pressed tightly to Pa's broad chest?

And what about Pa? The thought jolted her. So

many times she'd seen him grab Ma around her middle and give her a whirl. Or sneak up behind her in the kitchen, crushing her in a bear hug.

"Oh, Pa! I didn't understand," Cat whispered. "I didn't know how much you missed her."

A drop of rain slid down Cat's nose, and she frowned at the sky. The greenish tinge had faded, leaving a pale dreary gray that promised light showers. Hopping up from the bank, Cat brushed off the bottom of her overalls and snatched up the still fish. Then she marched back to camp, sincerely hoping that the men would be clothed.

"I was about to come looking for you," Raff greeted her.

Cat glanced about cautiously until she'd satisfied herself that it was safe.

"I told you where I'd be. Where's Wyatt?"

"Scouting."

"Oh."

"Want to rub my back again?"

"Does it hurt?"

"It's felt better."

Another rub would probably help, but with Wyatt gone, Cat felt wary. Not that she didn't trust Raff. But suddenly she didn't trust her own emotions.

"Keep your shirt on," she ordered, ignoring his grin.

If she'd hoped for a romantic interlude, an unveiling, Raff's actions kept her mood in check. As he sat on a log enjoying her services, he cleaned the fish she'd caught.

The fileted trout and mullet sizzled over the fire when Wyatt returned with news of the storm's damage.

"That twister cut a path through them trees 'crost the river, but this side jest got pruned of ol' limbs."

Cat flipped the fish in the iron skillet. "Are you going to clear the limbs tomorrow?" she asked casually, but her hopes leapt. Maybe the storm damage would delay them a day or two.

Raff, however, shook his head. "No need. When the felled limbs decay, the forest will be richer, Cat. In the meantime, it's a mess, sure. But it's not the same as having the rich topsoil scraped away."

She sighed, and perhaps sensing her disappointment, Raff clapped his hands heartily. "Hey, we've got some celebrating to do! We're safe, thank God! We have a good dinner frying. And there's a steamboat upstream."

Catching his enthusiasm, Cat hustled the men through their meal, sloshing coffee in the process. She could hardly wait to set foot on board the *Starlight* and only hoped the captain would permit a tour. But when they arrived, she hesitated. The well-frocked ladies and dapper men mulling around the deck would certainly think her a waif! And, worse, she'd have to agree.

"Well, what are we waiting for?" Raff asked when she halted.

"I . . . I don't know."

"Oh, I think you do. Feeling underdressed, huh? Now, don't go shooting those green dagger eyes at me. Take a good look at *me*."

For one thing he needed a haircut. Funny, she hadn't noticed before. And his palmetto hat, so practical on the river and in the heat, looked shabby in comparison with the top hats of the dashing men on board. But this was Raff, with his clear blue eyes and handsome face, and no one on the steamboat was as beautiful to Cat as he.

"Let's go," she said, grabbing his arm, and they boarded the *Starlight*, laughing, with Wyatt trailing close behind.

If eyebrows were raised at the sight of the conspicuous trio, expressions changed when Raff Jordan presented his family's respected name to the captain.

And tourists, from other states, other countries, who didn't know the Jordans, responded readily to Wyatt's warm chatter, listening appreciatively to his account of the storm's damage.

"That twister caused quite a stir," the captain told them, "but the panic was the worse of it. My crew had their hands full with swooning ladies and up-chucking gentlemen, so I'm much obliged for your report, sir. I expect we'll wait till daybreak to be off. You're welcome to stay until then."

With attention fastened on the men, Cat was free to wander about unnoticed, although she herself absorbed everything. Never had she seen such beautiful women so elegantly attired! With furs and feathers, velvets and brocades, even the plainest face or figure looked as though it had stepped from one of those fashion advertisements she'd seen in cast-off newspapers. What would it be like, she wondered, to dress so prettily and to parade with dainty steps and clicking heels?

Her own moccasined feet, however, padded through the boat's interior, wandering through the plush decor. A large cabin, centrally located, served as a lounge, cushioning weary travelers on velvet seats. In the middle of the floor lay a thick red carpet, patterned in an oriental design, and on the walls hung gold-framed paintings of exotic birds and wind-swept oceans. Overhead an enormous chandelier sparkled— a thousand stars clustered in the night—and Cat stood, neck craned, staring.

"Like it?" Raff asked softly behind her.

"Oh, it's beautiful," she answered, certain she was caught in a dream.

Shyly she ran her fingers across the velvet, touched the oil-painted canvases, and would have knelt to the rug if Raff hadn't stood, arms folded, watching her, amused.

Cat tossed her poorly capped head. "Is there a law against touching?"

He laughed. "Only if something breaks. Come on. I'll buy you dessert."

Away from the lounge, the dining room bustled with conversation and waiters, scurrying from passenger to passenger, carrying trays laden with various courses of a meal. Each table, swathed in white linen, glittered with crystal goblets and sterling silver, and Cat couldn't help gaping.

Standing in the doorway, she noticed that the men had taken off their hats as they dined, and since she couldn't do that, she reluctantly turned to Raff.

"I . . . I'm not hungry."

"What? No French pastries? No chocolate torte? No apple pie for you?" Raff teased.

"Apple pie?" Cat repeated wistfully. "Oh, let's get out of here!"

Fleeing to the deck, she found Wyatt, but Raff remained behind.

"A body could stifle with all them people, huh, Cat?" the boy said. "Now me, I like the river and lots of space."

"Did you wish you could be like those folks, Wyatt? You know—fancy and proper?"

"Cain't say I did. Them people's nice enough to folks as are friendly. But like I sed . . ."

"You like the river," she finished for him, smiling.

"I thought you two might be out here," Raff said, joining them. "Ah, good! The rain's stopped." He offered Cat a cloth-wrapped bundle. "I wouldn't want this to get wet. Well, don't just stand there," he chuckled. "It's not a bag of snakes!"

Timidly, Cat peeked beneath the cloth. "A whole pie! Raff! How did you manage that?"

"The chef was willing to part with it. It's apple."

"Oh, Raff!" Thankfully her hands were full or she would have been tempted to throw her arms around

59

him. "I haven't had an apple pie in eight years! Almost nine!"

"If you'll share it later, we'll feast on it in camp," he suggested. "That suit you too, Wyatt?"

"Huh? Oh, yeah, Raff. Shore." But the boy cocked his head, staring at Cat, puzzled. "I thought you wuz nine when yore Ma died. That'd make you nigh onto eighteen."

"Oh, I . . . I must have misfigured somewhere, Wyatt," Cat stuttered. "It seems like Ma's been gone a hundred years!" Then, brightly, she added. "Besides, I have a birthday coming up this month. Birthdays are so confusing!"

But neither of her companions looked terribly convinced.

CHAPTER 6

SHE'D HAVE TO BE more careful, she scolded herself, and suddenly Cat was glad the trip was almost over. Pretenses had never suited her, and lying came with great difficulty. Fortunately Raff and Wyatt pressed her no further, however, and both agreed to her suggestion of following the music that had sprung up from the lounge.

Inside the ornate room, Wyatt clapped his hands as the fiddler played, and since Cat refused to loosen her hold on the apple pie, she contented herself by tapping a foot. A woman with a cinched waist and bulging bosom swayed provocatively in a corner, and Cat wondered if the trussed figure and saucy yellow curls would gain Raff's attention. She peered at him askance, relieved that he took no more note of the woman than he had of others in the room. But when she saw Wyatt's open-mouthed stare, Cat almost giggled.

"Enjoying yourself?" Raff asked, smiling.

Cat nodded vigorously.

What fun it would be to stay on a boat like this, she

thought—to sing to real people instead of alligators! And what would Raff think if he saw her with flowers in her chestnut hair, wearing green silk to match her eyes or brown velvet to match her hair? She'd be as elegant as any woman there, and surely Raff wouldn't slap her flanneled back as he'd done just now!

"Quite a show," Raff said when the fiddling gave way to a banjo's tunes. "If you want to stay longer, Cat, you can, but the camp has been too long unattended." He shrugged apologetically

But Cat had seen enough for one night. Someday, she vowed to herself, she'd return, finely gowned. She just wished that Raff would be at her side.

Hospitably the captain bid them goodnight, and clutching her apple treasure to her middle, Cat loosened one hand in a farewell gesture.

"He seems like a nice man," she ventured, and Raff agreed as they started toward the dock.

Lost in her daydreams, Cat wondered if the captain might hire her to sing, properly attired of course, but her thoughts swerved when a rifleshot rang out, and she almost dropped her pie.

"What was that?"

"Gunshot," Raff said grimly. "You two head back to camp while I see what's amiss." Without waiting for a response, he wheeled around and took the small pier in two strides.

"Here, Wyatt." She shoved the bundle toward him. "Take this back for me. Please."

The boy scratched his head. "I dunno, Cat."

"You can have half! Just take the pie and go!"

Still he hesitated. "Raff sed you wuz to cum with me."

"I don't care what he said!" She stomped her foot. "If he's mad, it'll be my doing."

"Reckon it's yore neck," Wyatt said, disappearing into the shadows.

Keeping out of Raff's sight, Cat trailed behind, ears perked.

"No, no. No one's hurt." She heard the captain's reassurance. "One of the passengers shot a 'gator."

"For sport?" Raff demanded.

"I'm afraid so."

"I trust you're not sympathetic, sir, with the senseless slaughter of God's creatures?" Despite his polite words, Raff's tone was deadly. Cat sucked in her breath, praying there'd be no fight.

"Mr. Jordan, I respect your views on the matter, but you must understand my position," the captain said, equally firm. "Because of the cold winter, tourism is down, and I have to make a living. Antagonizing the passengers won't increase my trade."

"I appreciate that, Captain, but I've been led to believe that a man in your position has a say on what is or isn't allowed on ship. Will you, then, allow the slaughter to continue?"

The captain sighed. "I'll speak to the man. You have my word."

"As a gentleman, sir, that's enough."

To Cat's surprise, the two men shook hands, ending the exchange. Quickly she ducked into the shadows as Raff retraced his steps. His long legs strode past, and halted on the pier.

"Are you coming, Cat, or not?" he called over his shoulder.

Without answering, she followed him, bracing herself for his chastening tongue. But when he said nothing, the silence punished her disobedience far more.

"I guess you're angry," she said at last.

"I guess you're right."

"I didn't get in your way," she pointed out defiantly.

"No, but you eavesdropped. And you weren't safely in camp where I thought you'd be."

"Nothing happened."

"It could have!"

Suddenly she stopped, her own temper flaring. "What could have happened, Raff? What?"

"What difference does it make?" he shot back.

"Somebody might've been killed!" She was screaming now. "What would I put on your tombstone, Raff? 'This man died defending a dead alligator'?"

"I wasn't in that kind of danger, Cat." His voice, hushed and low, quietened her. "And I'm sorry you were frightened. But," he reminded her with a light swat on her backside, "you were supposed to be in camp."

The apple pie, which Wyatt had generously saved, proved a peace offering, and the three emptied the pan. Then, exhausted and content, Cat fell asleep by the fire.

Morning came early, with a new swarm of mosquitoes whining about her ears. Cat awoke, swatting. Her hands, her neck, her ankles sported welts, which itched more as she scratched.

"Is it all right if I kill mosquitoes?" she asked Raff peevishly.

"If they'll let you," he teased.

Trying to ignore the itching as Raff had suggested, Cat ladled their plates with grits.

"Why is it different?" she asked thoughtfully.

"What?"

"Why is it all right to kill mosquitoes and not alligators? Raff!" she suddenly exclaimed. "You killed a pig!"

Her shocked accusation amused him. Softly chuckling, he reminded her, "That pig provided barbequed pork and a new pair of shoes, Cat. I'd hardly call that senseless slaughter! A 'gator can provide food and a tough hide, too. It's killing for the fun of it that I object to.''

"Oh? Well, what about mosquitoes?" she asked smugly, thinking she'd trapped him in his own logic. "Just because they're pests. . . ."

Raff's amusement vanished. "Mosquitoes carry yellow fever."

She felt bad that she'd goaded him into the painful memory of the loss of his family, and feeling an apology would be inadequate, she simply said, "I didn't know."

But apparently Raff mistook her subdued response. "Don't worry, Cat. Most mosquitoes are relatively harmless. They only seem to inject you with a case of the orneries!"

She thought he was teasing again, but, growling, she barely refrained from throwing her plate!

Squirrels chattered as they scurried playfully across the live oaks that lined the river, and birds warbled prettily. From the raft, however, Cat, Raff, and Wyatt floated in dreary silence.

Earlier, the steamboat had chugged its way upstream, and the only reminder of its presence lay stiff and bloated, belly up from its final thrashing to escape the bullet's pain. Seeing it, Cat shuddered. A few yards away, another alligator lay dead, and this time, Cat's outrage equalled Raff's.

"The captain promised!"

Raff shook his dark head. "He only said he'd speak to the man, Cat, and I'm sure he kept his word. Unfortunately," he added drily, "people don't always obey the one in charge."

Irked at the barbed point Raff had made, Cat muttered under her breath. So he thought she was disobedient, did he? Well, she'd show him! She'd be so meek, so submissive, so quick to obey, he'd gag on her honeyed, "Yes, sir!"

Somewhat sullen from her own resolution, Cat made no comment when they passed the wind-toppled trees across the river. The tornado's destruction appalled her, especially since the twister had come so near. If it'd hit the water instead of the land . . . if it'd hit the opposite bank. . . . Both pictures evoked goose-bumped shivers. Why did God allow such disasters? And Raff had *thanked* Him that they'd been spared!

"I seen a twister once," Wyatt said unhelpfully, "that set a hen house in the neighbor's yard yet di'n't disturb even one egg in the nest! Mighty strange hap'nin's."

It was, indeed, and Cat would just as soon forget about it! When she'd hopped that train weeks ago, she'd thought of Florida as an enchanting land of sunshine and oranges and salt air. Instead she'd smelled mildew, been drenched in mild storms and had almost been killed by a tornado! Frost had killed the citrus but left the mosquitoes and snakes and alligators unharmed. And now the sun beat on her with moist heat until Pa's overalls and flannel shirt clung like wet, steamed mittens! Since this obviously wasn't heaven, she wondered just how far off track she'd come.

The mugginess dampened Cat's spirits more than Raff's barb. Yet she remained determined to carry out her resolution, responding to his requests with ready feet and verbal acquiescence.

Raff must have had other matters on his mind because they'd almost reached Siloam Springs before he noticed Cat's change in behavior.

"Hand me my boots, will you, Cat?"

"Yes, sir." She padded across to the fire where they'd been drying.

"Any more fish in the skillet?"

She nodded.

"Could I have some, please?"

66

"Yes, sir." She fetched the fish.

"Cat?"

"Yes, sir."

"If I asked you to fill the biggest kettle with boiling water, would you do that?"

Her shoulders slumped at the prospect of the horrendous task, but her determination didn't falter. "Yes, sir."

Sprawled on a log, Raff looked impressed. "You mean you'd stay up half the night hauling water from the river and waiting for it to boil simply because I asked you to?"

"I would!" she snapped, her temper finally getting the best of her. "You're in charge, remember?"

"I remember well. I just wasn't sure you did." In the firelight, Raff's eyes gleamed wickedly. "Well, what are you waiting for, Cat? Start hauling. I'm going to give you a bath."

She hesitated only a moment. "Yes, sir!" she said, refusing to give in. Then grabbing the half-cooled skillet, she declared, "I'll do it just as soon as you're prepared to meet your Maker."

Raff slid off the log, laughing.

"Oh, Cat! I'm going to miss you," he said when he could speak.

She set down the skillet, trembling. "What do you mean?"

"We'll reach Wyatt's house sometime tomorrow. I want you to stay there awhile," he said softly.

"I won't!"

Brushing himself off, Raff stood up and placed his hands on his hips. "Yes, you will," he stated firmly. "I'm in charge, remember?"

"Not if you leave me!" she said through angry tears. Turning her back, she fled toward the river.

"Cat! Cat! Where are you going?" he called after her.

67

Briefly her flight halted. "To take a bath! And don't you dare come near me!"

They arrived at the Tates' home after the next nightfall, and Cat was grateful for the dark that hid her reddened eyes. Feigning shyness, she hung back on the weathered porch, refusing to go in even when Raff came out to get her.

"I know you don't like this, Cat," he growled, so that only she could hear. "But I didn't expect you to be rude to Ma Tate."

"I'm not!" she exclaimed, stunned by his accusation. Rudeness was exactly what she was trying to avoid! Yanking her stocking cap down tightly over her ears, she racked her brain for a suitable explanation. Obviously her timidity hadn't fooled Raff one bit, but she couldn't tell him that good manners kept her outdoors with her hat on!

Something in his manner softened, and Raff himself provided her excuse. "I guess you'd fry indoors with those heavy clothes on."

"Oh, I would, Raff! And . . . and it'd be so nice to sleep out here on the porch swing." For emphasis, she plopped onto the wooden slats that were chained to the sloping roof. "Why, I haven't been on one of these since . . ." cautiously she stopped, before ending vaguely, "since I was little."

Raff peered at her oddly, his eyes sad and tender, and she thought he wanted to say something more. But "Goodnight, Cat," was all she heard, as he disappeared inside the cozy cabin.

Apparently Raff made her excuses well because Mrs. Tate wasn't the least offended. Immediately, she sent Wyatt out with a feather pillow to make their guest more comfortable, and as soon as the house quietened with sleeping children, she tiptoed out herself.

"Are you asleep, child?" she whispered.

Caught between daydreams and night, Cat cried

out, "Ma!" before she remembered where she slept. "Mrs. Tate," she corrected, sitting upright on the swing.

"Ma Tate suits me right well," the woman answered, sounding more like Wyatt than her own mother. Yet there was something comforting, something familiar, about her voice. "Kin I gitcha anything, son?"

"No, thank you, Ma'am," Cat said, suddenly feeling ashamed of her deception in light of this woman's kindness. She'd welcomed her and called her "son", and that deserved more than pretense. "I . . . I do need to talk to you, though."

"'Course you do, child. And there'll be lots of time fer that come daylight. You jest go back to sleep now. You must be plumb wore out."

She was, she knew, yet long after Ma Tate had gone inside, long after the house lay silent for the night, Cat stared into the darkness. Tomorrow she'd tell Ma Tate everything. Tomorrow she'd convince Raff to hire her as housekeeper or cook. Tomorrow she'd splash in Siloam Springs, her long hair free and flowing in the water. Tomorrow . . .

Finally she slept, dreaming of Raff. His hand lightly stroked her cheek. His lips softly brushed hers. He knelt beside her, warm and tender, calling her "kitten", saying he'd miss her, saying good-by. . . .

And when she awoke, frowning, he was gone.

CHAPTER 7

"THEY LEFT WITHOUT ME?"

Cat sat on the porch swing, rubbing her eyes against the threatening tears. How could Raff do this!

"It's best, child," Ma Tate consoled. "You're mighty welcome here."

"Oh, ma'am, I appreciate your kindness," Cat said, trying to pull herself together. "But I have to earn my keep, and . . . and you've got enough mouths to feed!" Her sweeping hand indicated the solemn little faces that peered at her shyly from porch and yard.

"I reckon I do," Ma Tate chuckled, unperturbed. "But Raff's been special kind to my family, and so's the Lord."

Uncertain what Mrs. Tate meant, Cat attempted her own explanations. "Helping me out doesn't repay Raff. I mean nothing to him!"

Ma Tate clucked her tongue, but if Cat expected censure of her honesty, it wasn't forthcoming. "Life's been hard to you, child, but I 'spect the Lord led you here to show His carin'." Settling her ample frame beside Cat on the porch swing, Ma Tate gave her a quick hug. "Raff thinks right highly of you. Wyatt, too. They sed they call you 'Cat,' but tell me. Is that short for Catherine?"

Gasping her surprise, Cat nodded her covered head. "How . . . how did you know?"

"Seein' you in the daylight. You're too purty to be a boy."

"I am?" Cat asked, even more astonished.

Ma's pleasant round face broke into a grin. "You shore are! Why, them eyelashes look like a crow's feathers, flying up and down a green pool. And yore little face is shaped like a heart." Incredulous, Ma Tate shook her head. "I jest don't understand how that boy of mine wuz so easy fooled."

"He wasn't!" Relieved by the lifted burden, Cat laughed. "You should have seen his face one day when I fussed at him to go find Raff! He said I sounded like you when one of the children is missing," Cat hurriedly added. "I had to be careful not to laugh aloud, too. But," she stopped, feeling ashamed. "I lied to him once when I said I'm fourteen. I'll be eighteen soon."

"Hit's a wonder he believed it," Ma said, chuckling.

"Not really." Cat said slowly as the thought occurred, "Wyatt is honest, and he expects that in others. I hope he won't be too disappointed when he discovers I've deceived him."

"Now don't be a-worryin' 'bout that. You had your reasons. To think! A girl travelin' alone." With a sympathetic cluck, Ma shook her head. "You want to tell me 'bout it, child?"

To Cat's own amazement, she found that she did want to tell everything to this compassionate woman, and with feet dangling from the porch swing, she slowly unfolded her tale—the changes after Ma's

71

death, the loneliness, the loss of Pa, the train ride, and even the strange feelings that Raff evoked.

When she'd finished, the Tate children had completed their chores. Ma, with much to do, sat quietly, listening. But the older woman's eyes had closed.

"Are you sleeping, Ma Tate?"

"No, darlin', I heard every word. I wuz jest askin' the Lord to come into every hurt and make it well." The clear eyes fluttered open. "Now! Tell me, child. Do I call you 'Cat' or 'Catherine'?"

"I'm used to Cat."

The sagging porch creaked as Ma stood up. "Then, Cat, I'm gonna point you to the rain barrel so's you kin wash up while I git them clothes on the line. Raff left you some money, and I 'spect you'll be needin' it fer a dress or two."

Cat shot from the swing. "No, ma'am! I don't want his money. You keep it. Please, I want you to. Pa's clothes suit me fine."

Ma looked at her oddly, squinting, as she cocked her head from side to side. "Reckon I might have somethin' else 'twould work. Though I 'spect you're a mite too small. Hmmm. We'll see." And with that mysterious promise, Ma Tate got out the washboard and filled the washtub on the porch.

When Cat had found the rain barrel hidden behind its private screen of shrubbery, she peeled off Pa's overall, stiff with dirt, and tossed them out for Ma Tate to wash. The odious shirt came next, and Cat wondered how she—or anyone else—had stood it for so long.

No more, she told herself as she lathered from head to toe with a cake of homemade soap. The suds felt good—reminiscent of long-ago nights when she'd soaked in a tub set in front of the kitchen stove.

"Scrub your neck and ears, Catherine," she could almost hear her mother say. Funny how the soft

72

foamy sounds and the sudsy smells evoked those memories she'd thought were buried.

She brought them out now, gladly, and she scrubbed until her hair, her body squeaked. How fresh she felt as she toweled herself dry! It was like she'd rid herself of a cocoon, ancient and shredded, in which she'd wrapped herself for lack of anything else.

Wearing a faded cotton dress, Cat skipped through the plain, unpainted house. She'd have to return the dress, which one of the Tate girls had loaned her, but for now it felt light and airy with her damp hair hanging low on her waist.

She wondered what Raff would say if he could see her—so feminine, so clean. Then she tried to convince herself she didn't care. But when she saw him again—*if* she saw him again—she vowed to give him a piece of her mind!

Meanwhile, the lively chatter and curious stares of the Tate children made it impossible for Cat to remain introspective. By evening she was caught in their after-dinner games of tag and hide-and-seek, rolling with laughter when Sara Ann found her hiding place and when she herself tagged the lanky, second-oldest, John. Certain she'd never had such fun before, she regretted the nightfall that bedded play and children much too early.

"Sing me a song, Cat, would you?" little Sara Ann requested when Cat tucked her in for the night.

"Old song or new?"

"A new 'un," the youngest said, delighted.

"Then close your eyes," Cat said, turning down the wick, "and I'll sing you a song as new as this minute."

Obediently two round eyes shut tight and, impulsively, Cat kissed the freckled lids. Then weaving her tale through a simple tune, Cat improvised, crooning:

When I was done growin',
the train was a-goin'.

I raced it. I caught it;
   I caught me a ride.
The train tracked the miles by,
with palm trees and blue sky,
passed river, slow rivers,
   slow rivers so wide.

The little eyes flew open. "Sing hit ag'in, Cat. Please."

Cat obliged twice more, then with a tickle to Sara Ann's ribs, said, "Enough now. Go to sleep!"

"Will ya make up a song tomorry 'bout when you wuz a little girl like me?"

"We'll see. Now go to sleep."

Cat tiptoed onto the sagging porch where Ma Tate waited.

"That wuz a mighty purty song, child. Seems to me like you got a gift from God fer singin' and makin' tunes."

"I never thought of it that way," Cat admitted, yet thinking about it now, she wondered if Ma Tate weren't right. The loving woman seemed to know a side of God that Cat had never experienced. "Do you think," she asked shyly, "that I could get a job singing—maybe to tourists?"

"I do fer certain," Ma Tate assured her. "That hotel down by the Springs wud be a fine place."

Cat nodded in the dark. Raff had told her about the hotel; so had Wyatt, and it sounded grand.

But now she sighed. "It's no use, Ma Tate. I'd have to have something fancy to wear, and," she added vehemently, "I am not going to use Raff's money!"

"Child, don't give up so soon," Ma Tate lightly scolded. "If the Lord gives you a gift, ain't He gonna make sure you git to use it?"

"I don't know," Cat answered honestly, and in the moonlight, she saw Ma's grin.

"Well, I know, child! And I know I got a couple fancy dresses from that Miss Augusta in town. She came out here a time or two with purties fer me 'n the girls, and I'll tell you true, Cat. I don't know why I kept 'em, 'cept maybe the Lord gave me a mind to."

"And you have them now?" Cat asked, excited. "The dresses?"

"That I do! Though we'll hafta take 'em in a mite."

Cat squinted through the darkness. "So that's what you were so mysterious about earlier!"

Ma chuckled. "Reckon I wuz. It'd been a spell since I'd seen them dresses, and I wanted to make shore the moths hadn't gotten 'em. I'd meant to show you after chores, but you wuz having sech a good time a-playin' 'fore dark, I di'n't have th' heart to spoil yer games. Sometimes a body needs ter be a child so's they kin grow up real good."

"Oh, Ma! How can I thank you for all you've done?"

But Ma Tate shook her head. "Don't go a-thankin' me, child. Thank the Lord. His gifts jes keep on a-givin' "

Curled again on the porch swing where Cat had insisted she preferred to sleep, she stared into the darkness long after Ma had gone into the crowded house. With new thoughts and excitement pressing on her, she'd never settle down for the night!

Perhaps Raff had done her a favor after all, abandoning her with the Tates. Surrounded by this cheery, loving family, Cat had seldom felt so hopeful, so light-hearted, so loved. Was it really God's doing, as Ma Tate had suggested? Had He given her a gift and then the means to use it? Tomorrow she'd find out!

When sleep finally came, the moonlight floated on the horizon, and in the east, fingers of light crept up the sky. Cat was sure she'd only dozed, but when she awoke, the bright sun glared.

"Saved you some biscuits and fried chicken," Ma

Tate said when Cat pattered, barefoot, into the kitchen. "But I reckon them cold grits ain't fit to eat."

Traveling the river, she'd had quite enough of grits anyway!

"I didn't mean to sleep so long," Cat apologized. Appreciatively she bit into the chicken, a crisp, golden breast.

"It's jest as well you rested," Ma Tate said, "cuz we've got to do some thinkin'."

Cat wiped her hands on the cloth napkin and waited for the older woman to go on.

"I wuz lookin' at them dresses ag'in, and I figure it might take several days to fit 'em proper."

Cat frowned. "That's too much work for you, Ma Tate."

"It's no sech thing, child, so don't be worryin' your head about that. It jest takes time, that's all. But time won't get you no fancy undies or button shoes like most ladies wear."

"I won't use Raff's money, if that's what you're suggesting."

"Didn't reckon you would, so I sent John on ahead this mornin' to the hotel to see if they'd be a-hirin' anybody."

"And are they?" Cat asked eagerly.

"Well, that's what we need to do some thinkin' about. They've got 'em a girl that sweeps and dusts and sech, but they need 'em a boy to wash up the kitchen."

Resolutely, Cat smacked the table top. "Then that's what I'll do!"

But Ma Tate wasn't so sure. "I jest don't feel right about it. You need ta be learnin' 'bout bein' a girl, Cat, so's you kin become a woman. There here paradin' as a boy don't set too well with me."

"I have to, Ma," Cat insisted. "I'm tempted to stay here, of course, but I want to earn my own keep. There'll be girls and women of all ages at the hotel, I

76

imagine, and I'll learn what I need to know, watching them. I promise. Besides," she gave Ma's plump hand a pat, "the only clothes I have are Pa's, and no one would hire a girl in overalls!"

"I 'spect yore right," Ma reluctantly admitted. "Oh, mercy, child. Sometimes it's hard a-knowin'."

As soon as Cat and Ma Tate had scoured the kitchen and taken turns rubbing sudsy clothes across the washboard on the porch, they set about altering the cast-off garments of Augusta Fairchild.

"Oh, my!" Cat said, eyes widening, when Ma brought in the two dresses, one of green silk, the other of white lawn. "Can you imagine anyone's not wanting these!"

"They are right handsome," Ma agreed, "but I 'spect Miss Augusta has all the gowns she needs, bein' a banker's daughter 'n' all."

"What's she like?"

"Same as most folks, I reckon, 'cept she talks real purty and smells nice, and she watches her manners proper like a lady."

Cat vowed to do the same.

"She must be tall!" she giggled as green silk dragged inches below her feet.

Ma tucked the hem, pinning. "Seems like a nice girl, too, though I've only met her once or twice when Raff brung her out."

"Raff knows her?" Cat asked, frowning.

"Now don't go gettin' jealous, child! Raff knows 'most ever'body 'round these parts."

Cat sniffed. "I'm not jealous," she denied. "Just curious."

When the gowns were pinned on almost every seam, Cat again bemoaned the amount of work Ma Tate would have to do.

"I don't know how I'll ever repay you!"

"The Lord takes keer o' that, darlin'," Ma graciously assured her. "'Sides, I 'spect I'll be right

77

pleasured working on these purty dresses." Suddenly the woman laughed. "Y'know, Cat, them gowns hain't no more fit fer dustin' and sweepin' than yore Pa's bib overalls! God shore do have a funny wit about Him."

Apparently that thought stilled Ma Tate's mind, and she insisted on accompanying Cat to the hotel to put in a good word for her.

"Won't hurt none, and might help," she said, settling the matter.

Before they left, Cat once again braided her hair and stuffed it beneath the stocking cap, but Pa's flannel shirt remained behind on the broader shoulders of a grateful John. Gladly the younger boy had traded two outgrown shirts that proved to be Cat's size, and she wore one of the lighter weight cottons now with the other tucked under her arm.

"Reckon the Lord knows what you need fer the work He's a-given you," Ma Tate said when the boyish Catherine reappeared.

"You know, Ma, I think you're right!" Cat said, grinning.

Sara Ann tagged part-way on the long walk, made longer by the glaring sun, to the hotel. But the little girl seemed oblivious to the heat as she skipped along perkily, begging Cat for another song. At first Cat responded readily, but she quickly discovered that the muggy heat drained too much of the energy required for walking. A few more songs, and she wouldn't be able to move a step!

Apparently, Ma Tate realized Cat's predicament. "Sara Ann, you've come 'bout far enough. Time fer you to be scootin' on home."

"But, Ma! Cat promised me a song about when she wuz a little girl!"

"Now, Sara Ann, I said we'd see," she reminded, but what she saw now was a crushed little girl! She hated for the child to be disappointed, but every breath was precious. With a questioning look, she appealed to Ma Tate.

"Tell you what. Let's set down here a spell an' rest, Sara Ann, and maybe Cat'll sing us a song. An' when she's done, you'll be a-goin' on home to tend yore chickens. Ain't that right?"

"Yes'm, hit shore is!" Obediently, the little girl plopped on the carpet of wild grass and dry leaves, waiting expectantly.

Cat laughed. Ma had a solution for everything, and somehow her cheerfulness made it easy to comply.

While she rested with knees beneath her chin, Cat thought of Sara Ann's chores and hers as a child, and a song about cracked eggs evolved. Twice sung, the silly lyrics and lively tune had the little girl giggling as she disappeared, chanting "No cake! No cake!" on the path home.

"Will she be all right?" Cat asked, staring after the child.

"Darlin', Sara Ann knows where her home is," Ma Tate assured her. "It's you I'm a-worryin' about."

They walked in silence then, a total of two miles, and when they reached the hotel, Cat quavered. What was she thinking of, going to a strange place like this, so huge, so grand, when the Tate family had warmly welcomed her, offering her a home? But no, she reminded herself firmly, she couldn't earn her keep there, and she wouldn't burden them for their kindness.

Straightening her shoulders, Cat marched past the large double doors, heading for a small side door that Ma Tate had indicated as the manager's office. Then, giving a sharp rap, Cat stood waiting.

From somewhere inside, a gruff voice called, "Come in," and Cat entered with Ma behind.

Her boldness faded when she caught sight of the man behind his desk. For a moment, she saw instead, the one who'd thrown her off the train! But this wasn't the same person, she realized, when he looked up at last, glaring.

"I hear you need a kitchen boy, and I've come for the job," she flatly stated.

"Cat'll be a good worker fer you," Ma Tate hurriedly added.

"Cat?" The man shot a stream of brown juice into a brass spittoon. "What kind of name is that?"

"Just a name," Cat said with a slight touch of defiance, "but if you don't mind it, I'll work hard, like Mrs. Tate said."

"Now Mrs. Tate, I've heard of," the man said a bit sarcastically. Then, "We'll see whether or not you'll do." Dismissing them, he looked back at the papers on his desk.

Uncertain, Cat lingered. "I have the job then?" she asked, and when he merely grunted, she revised her question. "Where do I report, sir?"

The small eyes snapped upward. "To the kitchen, where else?"

Outside once again, Cat exhaled a long breath. "Pleasant man, isn't he? I don't even know his name!"

Ma chuckled. "Mr. Smythe. My boys have helped him out a time or two, warshing winders and sech, and they sed he leaves 'em alone as long as they do their job."

"That suits me just fine."

With Ma Tate leading the way, Cat trailed toward a separate building that connected the hotel by means of a covered walk. Inside, the stale odor of grease assaulted her nose, and she squinted into the sudden dark.

At one end of the large room stood an enormous fireplace, big enough to stand inside, and across from it a long counter dipped midway into a sink. The other walls contained cabinets and expansive shelves for working, and next to one was a small man with snowy

80

white cap and a blood-stained apron. Cat assumed correctly that he was the head cook.

"My name's Cat, and I'm here to work," she said. " Mr. Smythe sent me."

"I'm Archy, and I wish you was stronger. The pump's outside the winder above the sink. Your room's behind that little door between them cabinets. You're expected to keep everything in here clean, including the floors and counters, pots and dishes. You'll be paid once a month if you stay that long." and with that, the frail man turned back to his own work.

Since everything appeared clean at the moment, Cat headed toward her room, curious about where she'd be staying. The space proved tiny, but, to her satisfaction, the corner spot contained windows on two walls, providing some ventilation and considerably more light than in the gloomy kitchen.

When she'd hung her spare shirt on the empty peg and tested the lumpy mattress, Cat proclaimed, "This isn't too bad," although she liked the porch swing better.

"Reckon you kin make out a month anyways. Lord willin', I'll have them dresses done long afore then." Ma's cheery face sobered. "Oh, Cat, I just hope we're doin' the right thing."

"We are, Ma! I've been thinking about it—being a lady and all, and I'm not ready for those fancy dresses anyway. By the time they're hemmed and tucked, I'll know how to wear them. I'm sure of it, Ma."

"I reckon you're right," Mrs. Tate reluctantly admitted. "Well, darlin', I'd best be gittin' home."

Cat sprang from the bed. "Oh, won't you see the Springs with me before you leave?" she pleaded.

It wasn't fair of her, she knew. Ma Tate had left her own work unattended too long, but Cat couldn't bear to see her go. And having the older woman with her when she visited the Springs for the first time would almost be like having her own mother there.

Tenderhearted Ma couldn't refuse the wistful plea. "Well, now I've been a-wantin' to see them purty Springs ag'in, and I reckon it'd be plumb foolish not to now I'm here. I'll jest take a quick peek 'fore I go." If Ma sounded as though she were talking to Sara Ann, Cat didn't mind.

Playfully she grabbed Ma's hand, swinging it, as she half-walked, half-skipped down to the Springs. But when she saw the water, the hand dropped, and so did her mouth.

"Oh, Ma!" she exclaimed, wonder-struck. "I've never seen anything like it!"

The placid surface shone like silvery-green glass that was splotched with bright aqua patches where the springs burst through the river bottom. Kneeling down for a closer look, Cat saw that wide-bladed grasses covered the sandy bed, like miles and miles of cut green ribbons dancing in the water. And the water! It was so pure, so clean, she could see rainbow-colored fish darting about.

Rolling up her pants legs, Cat waded out as far as she dared. The aqua patches fascinated her with their unusual beauty, but as she neared the source, her amazement grew. Millions of tiny bubbles spewed through the cavernous holes in the sandy crust, sending innumerable gallons of fresh water into the river's stream. Since no grasses grew around the aquifers, the incredible color of pure aerated water paused the reflected flow of silvery-green.

"Hain't it a sight fer sore eyes?" Ma said as Cat splashed toward her. "A body could stay here and look ferever if they didn' have little un's a-waitin'."

Cat knew it was past time for Ma Tate to go, and she braced herself for the parting.

"I'll always remember your being here with me

when I first saw the Springs," she said, hoping the words somehow expressed her thanks.

When Ma held out her arms, Cat went into them, wishing time would stop. But it didn't and, too soon, the older woman stepped back, her cheeks wet.

"I'll be a-prayin' fer you, darlin'," she said and was gone.

Shaken, Cat sat down on the sloping bank, soaking up the peacefulness and gaiety of the flowing river. Ma Tate was right. The patchwork beauty was a sight for sore eyes—and sore hearts.

When calmness had strengthened her again, Cat became aware of increased activity around the hotel. Her own rumbling stomach reminded her that others might expect a noon meal, and, for her anyway, that meant work! That was, after all, why she was here, she scolded herself as she rushed back to the cook-house.

No one seemed to have missed her, although a small stack of plates and an overwhelming number of sticky, crusted pans awaited her. At first she'd thought the coolness away from the fire was a blessing, but now she tried to figure how she'd get the boiling water in its heavy iron pot across the room. No wonder the cook had wished her stronger!

"Guess I didn't say you'd hafta keep water a-boilin' on the fire," he said to her now, and Cat expected it was the last time he'd do that job for her.

Embarrassed, she mumbled her thanks, wondering how she'd get the scalding pot down.

"Well, if you don't do something, this will be the shortest time anyone has held a job!" she muttered to herself. And with a determined heave, she snatched the water-weighted kettle from its stout hook.

There was no way, she decided wisely, that she could carry that thing to the sink without burning her legs! However, an ample-sized, thick rug near the hearth could serve her purpose. Careful not to slosh, she slid the steaming kettle onto the mat, and pulled, inched, her way across the room.

The awkward movement caught the indifferent cook's attention, and he grinned.

"Reckon what you lack in muscle, you make up fer in thinkin'," he said, and Cat beamed under the high praise.

It was the last pleasant moment of the day. Her arms ached from hauling and scrubbing. Her hands were reddened from hot water and lye soap. Her back hurt from lugging the kettle back and forth from pump to fire. And Archy fussed when the pan he wanted wasn't scrubbed when he wanted, and if she did so now, the greasy water would not be clean enough for washing plates! While she thought about it, the stack mounted, and the cook continued to complain!

Eventually the clamor of glass and iron and silver ceased, and Cat dried her chafed hands. What a day! She sighed before remembering that the evening meal was yet to come.

Unfortunately the dinner rush proved more taxing, and when it too had ended, Cat sank wearily into bed. Too tired to sleep, her mind raced over the events of the day. Was it only this morning that she and Ma Tate had seen Siloam Springs; that she'd sung to Sara Ann and said good-by; that she'd, dreamily, tried on green silk and white lawn?

Was it only yesterday that Raff had left without a word? Exhausted, she couldn't pretend, even to herself, that his leaving had not hurt. Unfamiliar shadows crept across the tiny room, but the black void inside herself was lonelier, emptier than a cavern underground, and, on the lumpy mattress, Cat curled herself against it.

Dark, oh, dark, the sudden night has fallen . . .

With nothing else to lull her, she waited for another day.

CHAPTER 8

"WHERE IS THAT MAN?" Cat muttered to herself for the hundredth time.

Over a week had gone by—ten days actually—and she'd still received no word from Raff. There was no reason she should hear, she reminded herself, except that she wanted to, but the fact that she didn't never ceased to annoy!

At least she'd been kept busy—not only at work but during her leisure time as well. She'd found a spot outside the hotel's main entrance where she could watch the ladies who strolled in and out without being observed herself. Then, alone in her room, she imitated their dainty steps and fluid movements.

Once, Archy had almost caught her talking to herself; after that, she'd been more careful. But even when she couldn't immediately practice a word, a phrase, a movement, she stored away every detail with the certainty that it would be of eventual use.

Meanwhile, however, she'd begun to tire of being alone, being on the outside. Certain that Raff and God

Himself had abandoned her, Cat set off to see the one person who'd not let her down.

She hadn't seen Ma Tate since coming to the Springs, so she'd awakened early, planning to spend this entire free day with the loving family. It irritated her that she'd missed seeing them her first day off, but no one had bothered to tell her she could leave until after the breakfast and noon dishes were scrubbed, dried, and put away! Unfortunately she'd never thought to ask.

Ma Tate, however, had needed time to finish the dresses, Cat consoled herself now, thus allowing a measure of forgiveness. How she hoped they'd be ready! If so, it'd truly be an occasion to celebrate—a special day, complete with layer cake.

Archy had baked the two snowy layers when she'd told him of her birthday. Of course, the date itself had passed, spent miserably alone, without Raff's remembering. But she'd wanted a cake to share with the generous Tates, and so, she'd hinted her request to the head cook the night before.

Although Archy had proved himself a kind enough man, Cat doubted that he usually baked for kitchen help. Perhaps he'd thought to make amends for her missed day off, and if so, the extra work was worth it, after all.

Lightly swinging the basket on her arm, Cat found the slender, tall magnolia that marked the path to the Tates. She wondered if she'd tire as easily as she had before, walking in the mugginess, but the earlier morning coolness and the days of laboring in a steamy kitchen with a kettle to lug soon quickened her steps. In no time, she reached the tin-roofed house, singing.

Sara Ann, the first to hear, came running, and Cat set down the cake and swung the little girl into the air.

"I shore did miss you, Cat!" Sara Ann said, plying her with wet kisses.

"Oh, I missed you, too!"

"What's that you brung?"

"A surprise," Cat whispered, "but don't tell anyone."

"Hain't got nuthin' to tell!" the little girl giggled.

The bigger surprise awaited still when Cat had greeted Ma and the rest of the family. As soon as the children had quieted, Ma Tate encouraged them to hurry to their chores so they'd have more time with their welcome guest. Not one of them dawdled! And when they'd gone, Ma motioned Cat into her small bedroom. There on the featherbed lay both of the dresses, shortened and tucked, and beside each was a pair of matching gloves.

"Ma! How did you do it?" Cat asked, astonished.

"'Member how you 'n' the girls wuz a-measurin' hands and feet to see whose wuz the biggest?"

Cat laughed. "And you guessed the size from that!"

Ma Tate nodded. "Best try 'em on to see if they fit. I reckon you'll be a-needin' 'em."

Looking at her reddened, rough hands, Cat grimaced. "Not exactly a lady's hands, are they?"

"May not look it, but they are fer shore."

Touched by that comment and Ma Tate's thoughtfulness, Cat's eyes watered. "I . . . I still don't know where you got the matching fabric," she sniffed.

"Well, child, that hain't nuthin' to cry about!" Ma teased, giving her a hug. "I jest pieced together what wuz a-gonna be thrown away from them shortened hems."

"Ma Tate, you're a wonder!" Cat exclaimed, admiring the snug fit of green silk about her fingers.

The dresses, too, hung nicely, as though they were made for her, and Cat twirled about, ecstatic. Both had full bodices, without darts or seams, which rose to a high-throated band, providing a perfect background for the locket Cat wore. The green silk, however, puffed in the back with a small bustle, and in the front spilled loops of wide satin ribbon.

The skirt of the white lawn flowed in simpler lines, saved from plainness by bands of wide lace. Lace trimmed the collar and the fitted sleeves below the elbow, but the unadorned upper sleeve ballooned fashionably.

"Reckon that's an hourglass figure, jest like they say," Ma Tate approved. "My, you shore look purty!"

"Do I?"

Cat wished she could see for herself, but the small, cloudy mirror only showed portions of each gown.

"Mercy! I 'most forgot!" Ma exclaimed as she bent down, peeking under the bed. "A lady's gotta have some fancy slippers, 'n' these here matched Miss Augusta's gowns. Hope they're fit fer walkin'."

Cat clapped her hands, delighted, then dropped onto a corner of the mattress to try on each pair. Both had wide satin bows, which she tied tightly. Even so, Cat stepped first out of the green brocade, and next, the white kid glove leather ones.

"Oh, Ma, it's no use! Miss Augusta's foot is longer than mine!"

"Child, you give up too soon. Take 'em off," Ma commanded, and when Cat had complied, the older woman stuffed a ball of fabric in the toe of each shoe. "Try 'em ag'in."

This time, the only obstacle was balancing successfully on tipsy heels, but once she'd accustomed herself to the height by walking back and forth across the room, Cat beamed, satisfied.

"These do look better than my moccasins," she decided, laughing.

"'Spect that depends on what yer wearin'," Ma chuckled. Suddenly she frowned. "Cat, hit weren't necessary for you to take that kitchen boy's job! You kin make out all right a'singin' with what you got now. I should've stuck to my guns 'stead of doubtin' what I knowed wuz best."

Flabbergasted, Cat took in what Ma was saying. Was, then, the back-breaking work at the hotel for nothing? Was the loneliness a mistake? Were the red hands an empty gesture?

No, she realized, she was learning to be a lady, and that, she knew, was necessary for herself. She'd also done what she thought best by trying to earn her own keep, by being a help at the hotel instead of being a burden on the Tates. Whether or not she needed the money she'd earned as a kitchen boy to finance her singing venture was irrelevant. She'd needed to earn her own way, and she had!

Ma Tate hadn't let her down by agreeing; nor was she letting Cat down now. The older woman simply had another perspective that didn't match Cat's own; yet both were born of caring.

Was that true of Raff too, she wondered. And Pa— misguided though his caring was? And what about those well-meaning ladies from the church back home? Were they wanting to be generous, without knowing how?

Augusta Fairchild was probably no different! Cat realized. The clothes she'd given Ma were worthless to the Tate family! *But not to me*, she thought. *Not to me. Not this time!*

All of a sudden, the inadequacies of people, of herself, seemed funny, and Cat rolled on the bed, giggling, until Ma Tate stood over her, shaking her head. She tried to explain, and when she'd managed sufficiently, Ma nodded, smiling.

"I 'spect most people mean well, child, though it may seem plumb foolish to others. Reckon we do whut's best fer shore when we do whut's lovin'."

Those words stayed with Cat on the path back to the hotel that afternoon. Her basket, emptied of cake and refilled with paper-wrapped shoes and dresses, swung lighter. And so did her heart.

How encouraged she felt by Ma and the Tate

children! After chores and a festive noon meal, she'd entertained them, slippered and gowned, with her songs. They'd all agreed on favorites, and she hummed them now, practicing once more for the interview she hoped to attain with Mr. Smythe.

As she neared the hotel, however, her confidence faded on sight of the grand place. And by the time she'd reached her small room adjacent to the kitchen, she'd almost decided to forget the whole thing!

"Child, you give up too easy." Ma's words came back to her. Steadied, Cat purposely remembered the excited faces of the children as she sang, her own joy in singing.

"God gave you a gift, so He'll make shore you git to use hit!" Ma had said.

"I guess I'll find out, won't I?" she told herself now. "But not without seeing Mr. Smythe!" Sighing, she shook the wrinkles out of the green dress.

Without the aid of a mirror, Cat coiled her plaited hair, more neatly she hoped, atop her head. Thus finely gowned, she peered cautiously into the kitchen as she cracked her bedroom door. Archy, a man of habit, had taken his usual midafternoon leave before the evening rush. And, Cat thought, if she'd calculated correctly, she'd have time to conduct her part of the interview with Mr. Smythe and return to her tiny room before Archy came back.

Sneaking out of the cookhouse undetected gave her another moment's pause, but once she'd hurried across the covered walk to the hotel, she slowed her pace, carefully mimicking the bridled steps of the ladies she'd seen around the grounds. As she neared the manager's door, her heart fluttered, but her gloved hand gave a bold knock.

"Who is it?" the familiar, gruff voice demanded at the intrusion.

"Catherine Caldwell."

"Who?" The door flung open with the question, and Cat repeated her name.

To her surprise, the hotel manager bowed slightly, and with a sweep of his arm, motioned her into his office.

"Now, what may I do for you, Mrs. Caldwell?"

"*Miss* Caldwell, if you please, sir, and I'm here in hopes of doing something for *you*." She sat, straight-backed, on the proffered seat, and briefly explained her mission.

"So you've come to sing for me, is that it?"

"Now, sir?" she asked, suddenly flustered.

Not knowing what to expect, Cat had merely envisioned a breezy chat and Mr. Smythe's saying, "Report to the lounge," much as he'd done before. But to sing for this man! And in his office!

"Well, what are you waiting for, miss?"

"I . . . uh . . . what song would you like?" she asked, trying to recover the air of confidence.

Thankfully Mr. Smythe's request was a tune she knew well, and without thinking about it further, she plunged in, filling the office with melody.

"Not bad. What's your price?"

"My price, sir?"

"How much do you want?" The man sounded impatient.

"Well . . . I . . ." she demurred, having absolutely no idea what to say since the terms of her wages had not occurred to her.

The manager apparently mistook her hesitancy for coyness, thereby bluntly stating a figure of his own.

"Oh, my," Cat responded when she realized she'd be earning twice as much singing as her kitchen job allowed.

"Not enough, eh?" the manager scowled. "Well, it'll hafta do until you've proven yourself."

Recovering from her shock, Cat regarded the man suspiciously. She had nothing to confirm the thought, no experiences, no comparisons on which to base her judgment, but something told her that he'd offered her far less than he normally paid an entertainer. This was, after all, a superior hotel!

Not wishing to jeopardize her new position, Cat found herself saying, "Very well, Mr. Smythe. The terms will do for now. However, I wish to be paid half in advance in order to supply myself with costume, and," she added more boldly, "I'll require a room in the hotel."

"Next you'll be wanting your meals free, I suppose!" But his tone suggested she dare not ask.

"No indeed, sir. Except," she added mischievously, "perhaps an occasional evening meal."

Grumbling, the manager tossed her a key and a small bag he'd filled with coins.

"You'd better be good, Miss Caldwell."

With a light curtsy, she made her escape before erupting into giggles. She'd done it! She'd convinced that impossible manager that she was not only a good singer, but a lady as well. And having accomplished that, Cat herself felt more convinced. The coins jangled with her amusement, and she silenced them against her. Never had she seen so much money! And by the end of a month, she'd have twice more! Wouldn't Ma Tate be surprised—and Raff!

Restraining her steps, Cat headed for the massive double doors of the hotel. As yet, she'd only been permitted a glimpse of the dining room through a back door when the serving staff had been short-handed. Celebrating now, she made her grand entrance through the front of the sprawling three-storied building.

Across a spacious foyer, a man looked up from the registry desk and smiled pleasantly as she entered. Cat ambled toward him with practiced steps.

"May I help you, Madam?"

"Why, yes, sir, I believe you may."

Showing him her key, she identified herself as the hotel's newly hired entertainer, then asked him directions to her room and the lounge.

"You'll find both just off the dining hall," he said, pointing to his left, and thanking him, Cat headed in that direction.

The small tapered heels of her shoes padded softly across the design of a muted red carpet, then clicked on the dark pine floor. The polished wood stretched throughout the dining area, which she entered through a wide archway.

Since she'd not had a proper look before, Cat paused, staring. Overhead hung chandeliers, tiered with rainbow-sparkling crystal, which caught the light from the tall windows. Each was elegantly draped with dark gold damask, tied back with golden cords, but snowy linens covered the round tables entirely.

Most of the Windsor chairs stood empty now, but here and there, people sat about, chatting.

"Lovely hotel! Simply lovely," one woman commented to companions.

Cat lingered as she walked by the table, taking in the ladies' clothes, their hair, their conversation and gestures.

"Aren't these pastries divine!" stated a lady of ample waist.

Archy would be pleased to hear that, Cat thought, and remembering him, she scurried toward the lounge.

Although it was still afternoon, the smaller room was darkened with shuttered windows and velvet drapes. Brass candlesticks stood around, instead of gaslights, and an unlit candelabrum rested on the piano. Next to the instrument, a small platform rose into a stage, and Cat scrambled up. Yes, this would do just fine.

Hopping down, she hurried through the archway that led to the corridor that bypassed dining room and lounge, and at the end of the hall, she found her room. Those for paying guests were on the upper floors that provided a grander view, quiet, and more ample space, but Cat was still impressed with her cozy corner.

A poster bed, draped with mosquito netting, stood against one wall, and beside it, a covered table held a rose-colored lamp. Two long, narrow windows, curtained with rose-flowered chintz, offered light on the end wall, and on the wall adjacent was a wardrobe, plain in design, yet large enough to hold several gowns. An oak washstand provided additional storage, and atop it sat a china pitcher and bowl and fresh linens. What luxury! Cat thought, as she stepped across the hooked rug of primrose color and pattern.

It was then that she spied the mahogany-framed mirror, tall and tilted on its stand. Closing the door to her room, she patted her hair, smoothed her skirt, and stepped cautiously toward the glass.

Enormous green eyes, feathered with long, dark lashes, stared back, wide-eyed. High-boned cheeks, which flushed becomingly, set off her slender, straight nose, and the rose-tinged lips smiled at her shyly.

"My goodness," she said.

The picture she presented was too old-fashioned, she realized, but there was no time now to make adjustments. Archy would return soon, and getting past him was not as simple as maneuvering around others on the kitchen staff.

Hurriedly Cat stuffed the bag of coins beneath her bed pillow, and pausing only to relock the door, she hustled toward the cookhouse. She entered it breathlessly, and immediately she clapped her hand across her mouth as Archy's supposedly unknown name erupted from her lips.

"Goodness, sir, you startled me!" she said, attempting to cover her mistake. "I was told that no one was here, so I came to have a look around. I'm Miss

Caldwell, and I'll be entertaining after supper hours at the hotel. You, of course, must be the head cook. Don't mind me, please. I'll have my look and be off.''

As she'd hoped, the typically quiet Archy didn't know quite what to make of her as she flitted about the kitchen, gushing interest. Another flutter of silk took her to the door of the kitchen boy's room, and before Archy knew what to say, she'd glided in, snatched up her overalls, moccasins, and one shirt, leaving the other on its peg. She stuffed the bundle under the paper-wrapped clothing, and glided out again, the basket concealed behind her bustled back.

"I must say! You do keep a spotless kitchen," she effused. "And your pastries are *divine!*"

"Thankee, Ma'am." The red-faced Archy beamed as she waved a quick good-by.

When she'd entered her hotel room again, Cat leaned against the door, shaking with laughter. Perhaps this double life would not be as difficult as she'd feared, and for now anyway, it was fun.

As soon as she'd hung her scanty wardrobe and assured herself that her bag of coins remained untouched, she investigated every drawer and nook for a safer hiding place. She found none to her satisfaction, but she did discover various items left behind by former occupants of the room: a scattering of hairpins, a man's handkerchief, a half-used rouge pot, and a lace fan in remarkably good condition.

Cat promised herself a trip into town when she knew what else she'd be needing. But now, she pivoted in front of the mirror, studying herself critically. Her trim but nicely rounded figure pleased her, but she gave it little attention as she noted instead that dratted bustle. None of the ladies she'd observed seemed to be wearing them except one elderly woman who'd also defied fashion by coiling her hair around her ears.

Unbraiding her own chestnut hair, Cat smoothed it

with her makeshift comb then pinned it in a light twist, which seemed to be the style. The effect was still too severe, and she wrinkled her nose in distaste. How had the other women achieved their softer look, she wondered? Closing her eyes, she tried to remember.

Curls—or at least a fringe of short hair—framed the faces, she recalled. Without another moment's hesitation, she located Pa's knife and set about, trimming. The result was miraculously feminizing as the humid air did its work in springing soft waves about her face.

The coiffure, however, made her pink-sprigged gown of green silk appear even more old-fashioned. *It's no use*, she told herself as she dropped onto the tapestried seat of the one chair in the room. But Ma Tate's words chided gently.

"Child, don't give up too soon."

"It's no use!" she repeated aloud. "Unless . . ." the thought came to her, "unless I purposely costume myself!"

The idea, she thought, was splendid, and she completed it artfully as she coiled a braid around either ear. Thus coiffured and attired, Catherine Caldwell made her stage debut.

CHAPTER 9

A FEW DAYS LATER, lugging her kettle from pump to fire, Cat wondered what she'd gotten herself into! Constantly exhausted from late hours in the lounge and early ones in the kitchen, she questioned how long she could maintain her charade. To make matters worse, the manager had caught the kitchen boy slipping out of Catherine's room!

The thought worried her now, not so much for her own reputation, but because she had no doubt that Mr. Smythe would carry out his threats to give the boy a hiding! Perhaps she could placate the man with a visit, explaining that Cat was a relative. No, that might make the manager too suspicious. She could tell him that she was teaching the boy to read. Or sing! That wouldn't be a lie.

How she detested these deceptions! She only hoped she could maintain her dual roles until payday at the end of the month. Two weeks away! The thought exhausted her further.

Still, she knew she needed the money to outfit herself properly. A brief excursion into town had proven that. How quickly her coins had flown into the shopkeeper's hands! But she'd needed the summer-weight hosiery and nightgown with its shirred front. Instead of buying the less expensive one-piece combination garment, which would have been impossible beneath Pa's overalls, she'd selected cotton drawers and a French chemise, tucked at the waist.

The pink ribboned collarette, she could have done without, but it matched her delightful discovery of pink brocade walking shoes that fit her well. By fastening the collarette on the throat of the white dress, the pink shoes suited both gowns, and so did the pink-plumed aigrette that she'd purchased for her hair.

Reluctantly she'd passed up the pink ruffled parasol and the dusky rose gown that had seemed tailor-made for her when she'd wistfully tried it on. At the time the extra dress would have taken almost all of her remaining coins, and she'd felt certain the purchase could wait until the month's end. Now she wasn't so sure she'd survive that long!

With her hands plunged in dishwater and her mind drowning in dilemma, Cat scarcely heard the shuffle of boots.

"Cat?"

Sloshing suds, she wheeled around. "Raff!"

How handsome he looked with his fawn-colored cord breeches and tucked shirt! His freshly trimmed hair enhanced his dashing appearance, and those eyes, those incredibly blue eyes, twinkled.

"I thought you'd be mad at me."

"I am!" she said, remembering. "You went off and left me at the Tates'—as though they needed another mouth to feed!"

"Your care was provided for; you had no need to worry."

"As if I'd take your money!" she spat.

"So I heard." For some reason, he seemed

amused. "And now you're scrubbing dishes and fattening yourself on hotel food."

"I'm not fat!" she denied while not resisting the urge to check her derriere.

Raff laughed heartily. "Oh, Cat, I have missed you!" he chuckled.

"Hmmpf!" She turned back to the well-soaked breakfast plates. "You could have said good-by."

"Good-bys between friends are too hard," he said softly. "Now, when are you going to ask me what I've been doing?"

"Maybe I'm not interested."

"Don't pout. It doesn't become you," he scolded. "But I'll tell you what I've been doing anyway."

At first she pretended not to listen as he told her once again about the devastated land, struck first by prospectors and more recently by frost. Ironically his father's early investments in phosphate had left Raff financially comfortable. But until he used part of that money to reseed the damaged land, he'd never feel comfortable with himself, his own conscience.

"It's not that I'm against phosphate mining," he explained, "but the carelessness was inexcusable. Most of the damage is to the north of here, toward the west. With four hundred mining companies in existence at one time, you can imagine how much destruction their ill-trained men could do. Or maybe you can't," he added suddenly. "Would you like to come with me, Cat? There's one bad area not too far from here."

The suggestion tempted her, not because she wanted to see for herself, but because she'd enjoy the excuse of accompanying Raff anywhere. Somehow, however, that seemed like another deception, and those had proved too taxing already.

Reluctantly she shook her head, declining.

"I see," Raff said, his voice cold and distant. "I

thought you'd be interested by now, but apparently I was wrong."

"No, you weren't! I am interested," she said, realizing it was true. Strange and exotic though Florida was, she'd come to love the land, and it troubled her greatly that her father had almost participated in the heedless, greedy search. Perhaps the proceeds from Ma's brooch had been better spent where less harm was done. At least Cat still had the locket.

"It'd be too hard to get away," she told Raff now. "Besides . . . I don't like seeing things torn up."

He eyed her suspiciously. "You're not still annoyed with me for a foolish mission?"

"What?" she retorted before admitting to herself that she had felt that way. And Raff had noticed! In fact, he seemed to care what she thought.

Slinging suds from her reddened hands, Cat wiped them dry on her breeches. Then facing Raff, she told him, "I don't have to see the land to know it's bad if you say it's bad! And you wouldn't be involved in this . . . this reseeding project, if you didn't think it was important. So don't you get huffy with me just because I don't snap to your heels when you decide to remember I'm around!"

The blue eyes sparkled, and she knew he was laughing at her.

"Cat!" he exclaimed. "I do believe you're beginning to trust me."

"Did I say that?"

His handsome head nodded. "You've trusted my judgment, and that's a start."

He talked on for a while about the phosphate companies, assuring her that the ones in existence now had reasonably well-trained staffs that might make future seeding projects unnecessary.

"What about your own land?" Cat asked, curious. "I thought you'd be top-working your groves."

He smiled at her knowledgeable interest. "Wyatt's in charge there, rounding up a crew which I'll be ready to oversee in a few days."

"A crew!" She flung down her dishcloth. "You turn me out, then hire a whole crew?"

"Don't go getting your dander up! I wasn't sure what help we'd need until I'd surveyed the grove myself, but, as I'd expected, Cat, we need strong arms and stout backs."

"I have both," she insisted hotly.

To prove her point, she unhooked the heavy iron kettle from its place above the fire, then expertly, she scooted the burdened mat across the room. Midway, however, her triumphant look faded as Raff seized the wooden handle and, without a word, carried the steaming kettle, effortlessly, to the sink.

"Is this where you want it?" His questioning smile mocked.

Furious, she stomped her foot. "I don't need your help!"

"Nor I, yours," he retorted with sarcasm.

Knowing he was right, she turned her back on him and stilled her quivering lip. Oh, why must they always be at cross purposes? she wondered. Why couldn't they simply enjoy one another's company as she so wanted to do?

Coming up behind her now, Raff clasped her shoulders, and the touch sent tiny arrows of warmth shooting into her very core.

"Tell me, Cat. Are you unhappy here?" His softened voice sounded tender.

She felt limp from his closeness, but vigorously she shook her covered head in response, shaking away, too, the sudden giddiness.

"I have a good job, good food, and a good place to stay," she assured him as she mindlessly washed the same spot in a dish. "The pay isn't bad, and I can visit the Springs every day. The Tates aren't far either."

"They look forward to your visits," Raff said casually, and she stiffened beneath his grasp.

Had Ma said anything to him? Had the children? Cat didn't think they'd give away her secret, respecting instead her right to tell Raff in her own time. But how could she tell him? she wondered. What would she say? *Oh, by the way, Raff, I'm an eighteen-year-old woman!*

"I saw John this morning, wearing your flannel shirt," Raff told her now. "I'm glad you worked out a swap—you'd be sweltering otherwise—but if you need another, I'll be going into town Friday."

"No, thanks," she said. "I have two lightweight shirts. And besides," she added mischievously, "I might be in town Friday myself."

The more she thought about it, the better she liked the idea, and over the next few days, she amused herself by envisioning the scene. She'd wear the white dress and pink collarette because it was more fashionable and because, she'd noticed, when she wore it on the stage, the men in the audience responded with noisy enthusiasm. That had proven to be such a problem, in fact, that she'd taken to wearing her old-fashioned costume almost exclusively onstage. She'd even told the hotel staff that she was in need of additional costumes, and one or two had promised to search their retired wardrobes for hand-me-downs.

How she wished she'd been able to afford the brand-new gown of dusky rose! But the white lace-banded dress would do, and she could hardly wait to see Raff's face. She could almost see it now, mingled with shock and delight, as she introduced herself.

"Good morning, Mr. Jordan," she'd say as those clear blue eyes studied her quizzically, wondering where he'd seen her before. And when he asked, she'd tell him, "I'm Catherine Caldwell, sir. But my dearest friends call me 'Cat'." Oh, the look he'd give her then before sweeping her into his arms!

By Thursday night, she'd played out the scene a hundred times in her mind, treasuring it with more and more excitement. She'd even managed to trade days off by promising Archy she'd return before the evening meal—not exactly a bargain for a full day's work Wednesday, but Friday nights were busy. She knew Archy needed her help, and she had no desire to jeopardize her job.

Content, then, with the prospect of a free day coming—and such a promising one at that—Cat sang out her joy and pleasure that night in the lounge. The audience, which was comprised mostly of men, responded to her warmth with thunderous applause. Their appreciation took her by surprise, and impulsively, she blew kisses from gloved hands. How happy she felt! And not one man had acted ungentlemanly toward her.

Despite the lateness of the hour and her wish to be abed, Cat couldn't refuse her appreciative audience a final encore. She dropped into a deep curtsy on the last note while the men rose, cheering. Overwhelmed, she left the stage quickly, to pause beneath the archway of the lounge in a dramatic farewell gesture. The men loved it! And, if possible, their applause rumbled louder.

"Marvelous performance!" said a voice behind her, and, startled, she jumped.

"You frightened me!" she said, clasping her hand to her bosom.

The tall blond gentleman gallantly bowed his apology, and Cat couldn't help smiling. She'd seen him often in the lounge, and she'd guessed him to be alone on a holiday. His introduction, however, proved her wrong.

"Forgive me for startling you, Miss Caldwell. I'm an avid fan of yours, and frightening you was not my intention."

"What is your intention?" she asked innocently.

103

His swift glance, from coiled braids to brocade toes, alarmed her before he answered, "I merely wished to introduce myself if you'll permit me." Again came that gallant bow. "I'm Lloyd Fairchild of Siloam Springs."

Immediately Cat hoped her stunned expression had not portrayed her shock. Then recovering herself, she extended a hand.

"Mr. Fairchild. I've heard of your family, though I've yet to meet them."

"Perhaps we can remedy that soon." To her amazement, he pressed her gloved fingers lightly to his lips. "Tomorrow?"

She snatched her hand away. Then, not wanting to appear ungracious, she informed him, "I've made prior arrangements for shopping. Besides, Mr. Fairchild, you must admit we've scarcely met!"

"Have we now?" He seemed to consider that. "I've so enjoyed your performances that I feel I've known you for some time. I certainly wish that it were so!"

Charmed by his flattery, Cat softened somewhat. His was certainly a reputable family, and she'd given many a thought to Miss Augusta, wondering just how attractive Raff found the girl—though she could hardly be called a girl, if the tall, voluptuous form of her dresses was any guide!

It would be interesting, Cat thought now, to discover more about the Fairchilds. Usually she discouraged the men who sought her after a performance, but Lloyd was different. Raff knew his family, and so did Ma Tate. No, she decided, she wouldn't discourage Lloyd Fairchild.

"We'll meet again soon, I'm sure," she said, bidding him good night.

But the tall young gentleman was in no rush to see her go. "Forgive me if I'm being presumptuous, Miss Caldwell, but since you're occupied tomorrow, I wonder if you might consent to accompanying me now. Ah! I've shocked you again—how crude of me—but I'm merely suggesting that you share a glass of wine with me before you retire."

"Really, Mr. Fairchild! It's quite late," Cat insisted, hoping she wouldn't have to be rude, "and I don't care much for wine."

"Coffee then. And, yes, I realize the hour, Miss Caldwell, but it's not so very late, and the *Starlight* doesn't dock often."

"The *Starlight?*" she asked before she could stop herself. "It's . . . it's here?"

"For a few days, I imagine. Don't tell me you didn't know."

But she didn't know, having had little opportunity for leisure that afternoon. Apparently the steamboat had arrived hours earlier, stopping over to gain part of the tourist trade about the Springs as it did occasionally when travelers were scarce.

What good fortune its arrival could bring! As much as she hated to admit it, Cat knew that her feelings for Raff were not necessarily reciprocal. The thought had even crossed her mind that he might not like his young friend to be whisked away, replaced by a slip of a girl. He might not think her attractive. He could be angered at her deception. His heart could be elsewhere. . . . Oh, so many things could go wrong!

Chewing her lower lip, Cat hesitated until Lloyd's comment made her decide.

"What do you have to lose, my dear? An hour or two of sleep? Come with me."

How could she refuse, especially when to do so would be foolish! She'd longed to board the *Starlight* dressed in finery, and for a moment, she lamented her old-fashioned gown. There was no time now to change, and if she suggested they wait until the morrow, Mr. Fairchild might himself decline. Besides, she preferred her quaint costume for performing, and, should the opportunity present itself tonight for her to sing for the captain, she wanted to be ready. What better time than the present—especially since she had a willing escort! And so, Cat took the arm that Lloyd Fairchild offered her, wondering if this opportunity were God-sent.

As they approached the steamboat, which was docked within easy walking distance of the hotel, Cat exclaimed that it did indeed look like starlight. She'd forgotten what a dazzling spectacle the lanterned torches made, their quivering shafts of light shooting upon the water.

The captain welcomed them aboard, greeting her companion with warm recognition.

"Good to see you again, Mr. Fairchild, and your lovely miss."

"Lovely indeed, sir! You should hear her sing. But I'm forgetting my manners, captain." Briefly he made the introductions.

"Ah! You entertain at the hotel, then?"

"Yes." Cat nodded demurely, giving a slight curtsy as she'd seen other ladies do. "I'm afraid, sir, you've caught me still in costume," she said, knowing full well the choice was hers, but hoping he'd take the hint.

He did. "Would it be an imposition to ask you to give us a song or two?"

"Oh, no, sir. Not at all." Then, frankly, she admitted, "I've dreamed of singing aboard the *Starlight*."

A puzzled frown creased the captain's forehead, and Cat prayed she hadn't been too blunt. But he was, it seemed, merely trying to place her.

"You've been aboard before?"

Instantly Cat stopped the denial that sprang to her lips. Both of these men had been kind, and she had little stomach for lies. Unable to answer truthfully, however, she avoided a direct response.

"I've often admired the *Starlight* from the shore."

"So have we all," her companion agreed as he guided her, firmly but steadily, toward the lounge.

When they'd been seated, Lloyd leaned forward, confessing, "I'd rather hoped to have you to myself tonight. As soon as you've sung, that will be an impossibility, I fear."

"Then I shall wait until we're ready to leave," Cat assured him, smiling. It wouldn't do to offend her escort. "Now, tell me about your family, Mr. Fairchild."

"Lloyd, if you please. And, if I may be so bold to ask, may I call you 'Catherine'?"

Uncertain of proprieties, Cat hesitated until Lloyd took the matter into hand, thereafter referring to her as "Miss Catherine."

He spoke her name often, caressing it, as he talked of himself and his sister, Augusta, but when Raff's name failed to enter the conversation, Cat couldn't suppress a yawn.

"I'm boring you," Lloyd stated with a note of regret, and Cat hastened to assure him that she was merely tired.

"I do have a full schedule tomorrow," she reminded him, and reluctantly Lloyd agreed that the evening should end.

Lloyd gained the captain's attention with a prearranged signal, and the moment Cat had been waiting for arrived. Since many of the lounging tourists had heard her sing earlier, she was welcomed with warmth. A quick glance at the chief officer's face revealed that he, too, was pleased.

Since the only accompaniment available was a banjo, Cat showered the audience with a lively folk tune and another, her fatigue forgotten until Lloyd's lifted eyebrow reminded her. If he hadn't already assured her that he was an avid fan, she would have thought him disinterested as he offered his arm in parting. But the rest of the crowd more than made up for his coolness.

"That was delightful, Miss Caldwell," the captain said as he accompanied the couple across the moonlit deck. "I hope you'll come again."

"Perhaps to dine," Lloyd answered for her as if to close the matter of her singing there again. He had not taken into account, however, Cat's own determination.

"I'd love to entertain your guests another time," she said, ignoring her escort's grimace. "Tell me, captain," she added recklessly, "would you consider hiring a singer to travel with the *Starlight?*"

"If that singer were you, Miss Caldwell, I'd be honored."

"Then I'll let you know when I tire of the hotel," she promised with a smile.

"The hotel or that ogre of a manager?" the captain asked impishly, and Cat couldn't help giggling.

When she and the captain parted, still laughing, Cat saw that Lloyd was not amused. Rather sullen, he walked her back to the hotel without speaking. Untroubled by his silence, Cat supposed he was sulking, but she thanked him for the evening and said a pleasant good night.

"Miss Catherine, wait!" He delayed her as she prepared to enter her room. "Would you . . . would you really accept employment on a . . . a steamboat!" He sounded aghast.

This time Cat had no qualms about proprieties, no concern about rudeness. Stretching herself full height, she answered coldly, "I should be quite pleased to entertain on the *Starlight*, Mr. Fairchild, and so would you if you had no source of income other than your own devices. My father was not a banker."

And with that, she slammed the door in his astonished face.

CHAPTER 10

SHE AWOKE THE NEXT MORNING feeling unrested and angry, and it didn't help that someone was beating on her door!

"Who is it?" she snapped. One of the maids with a message from Mr. Smythe stood before her, her eyes wide with surprise at Cat's unfriendly tone.

"No'm, I don't know what it's about," the girl insisted when Cat asked, "but he's upset about something, for sure, and says you're to come right away."

"I'll do that, thank you. And, Miss . . ." Cat handed the girl one of her precious few coins. "Would you ask the cook's helper to wait for me? He'd promised me a ride to town this morning, and I'm sure I shan't be long."

Cat hurried through her toilette, splashing water on her face and vigorously brushing her hair. Lightly she twisted the thick mane and pinned it on the crown of her head, stabbing herself in her haste. A feather of curls framed her face, and in front of either ear, a longer ringlet dangled. Satisfied, she slipped into her dress, and fastened the pink collarette around her neck.

She allowed herself a critical moment in front of the mirror.

Too pale, she decided, then felt annoyed again that she'd had so little sleep and was rushing now. She'd so wanted to look her best for Raff, but there simply wasn't time.

She'd started for the door when she remembered the rouge pot, and she stopped on the primrose rug, wavering with indecision. Perhaps a dab, she told herself. Having nothing else with which to apply it, she touched a finger to the deep pink color and wiped it carefully across her mouth. Pleased with that improvement, she added small patches to either cheek and instantly wished she hadn't. The dots of color looked too unnatural, and she certainly didn't want Raff Jordan thinking her a trollop!

Impatient to be off, Cat seized the man's handkerchief she'd found, and, hoping it was clean, she patted the color from her face.

"Oh! That's better!" she told her reflection, which smiled at her with darkened lips and just the lightest hint of blush.

Moments later, however, she stood in the manager's office with cheeks aflame.

"You heard me, Miss Caldwell! If you sing on that boat again, you're fired! I won't have them stealing away my business with an entertainer from my payroll. Do I make myself clear?"

"Most assuredly! But Mr. Smythe, it never occurred to me that the hotel lounge would lose business *after hours!*"

"I'll thank you to keep your tongue, Miss. I've said my piece, and I'll stick by it."

"Very well, Mr. Smythe, that's your privilege," Cat said in what she hoped was a more respectful tone, though the man had done little to deserve it.

Seeing that she'd been dismissed, she made her leave, but paused at the door. "I'm curious. Not that it was any secret, but I'm wondering how you knew I'd sung last night on the *Starlight*."

Hunched over his desk, the manager didn't bother looking up. "I have my sources," he mumbled.

All the way into town, Cat stewed, convinced one minute that Lloyd Fairchild had been responsible for the morning's lecture, then certain the next that he wouldn't possibly have caused her such trouble. Or could he? He seemed determined to prevent her singing on the steamboat again.

But no, she reminded herself, he'd only wanted the assurance of her undivided attention. Surely he wished her no harm. She'd made it clear to him that she had to earn her living as best she knew how, and he couldn't hold a grudge against her for that, could he? Perhaps he could. She'd said some rather unkind things to him, she recalled, blushing—even hinted that he was too lazy to work, contenting himself instead with his father's money! In broad daylight, she could see how that might not set too well.

Still, who did he think he was? Coming into her life, uninvited, placing expectations on her. "How dare he!" she muttered beneath her breath. And when the hotel buggy arrived in town, Catherine Caldwell had little need of a rouge pot to heighten her color.

Having arranged time and place to meet the cook's helper, Cat descended from the buggy and immediately wondered where to go. She'd almost forgotten the purpose of her visit, and it occurred to her now that she had no idea where Raff intended to shop or what business he had to conduct. Not that the town was so large, but it would be difficult to bump into someone at the opposite end.

Since the dry goods store and general mercantile were adjacent, both overlooking the bank's brick face, Cat sauntered in that direction. She crossed the broad street, lined with palms that provided little shade, and stepped onto the wood-planked sidewalk, heels clacking. Thankfully, awnings stretched from the top edge of each large window, casting cool shadows. Still, Cat wished for a parasol to block the midmorning sun. She wondered idly if the pink ruffled one were available, and if so, would the price seem as high as it had that first day of shopping?

A glance up and down the sidewalk and across the street showed no familiar faces, and Cat stepped into the dry goods store with a sigh. The pink parasol on a shelf behind the ready-to-wear dress rack was easier to find than Raff, and she passed bolts of cloth and beaded bags, heading toward it. A price tag fluttered from the pink handlegrip, but the cost hadn't altered. Cat turned away, catching a glimpse of the deep dusky rose gown she'd so admired. Funny that it should cost only slightly more than the parasol.

She supposed the dress had hung too long on the rack, or perhaps the cotton muslin had some flaw. But a close inspection of the narrow skirt and accordion-pleated front bodice proved the fabric and seams intact. The color, she decided. Dove grays and creamy beiges seemed to be the rage, but Cat didn't care. The other ladies could wear muted shades if they desired, but she wanted that rose dress!

Knowing the gown would take every cent she had, Cat forced herself to walk away. Leisurely she browsed among the shelves, several times declining the fawning attentions of the clerk. He was beginning to get on her nerves!

Where was Raff anyway? Had she misunderstood when he'd said he'd be in town Friday morning? Had he come early, rapidly taken care of his business, and gone home? Despite her own delays, she'd arrived shortly after the shops had opened, but perhaps she'd missed him while she lingered over the rose gown.

Restless she paced in front of the shop window,

112

casting glances in every direction, and at last she spied a familiar figure, trim in a dove gray suit, coming from the bank.

"Lloyd!" she called to him from the covered walk. A few heads turned and, with lifted brows, chastized her unladylike behavior. But if Lloyd himself minded, he gave no clue as he strode toward Cat, beaming.

"Miss Catherine! You'd said you'd be in town today, but I'd hardly thought I'd have the good fortune of running into you."

Feeling foolish at unwittingly having made a spectacle of herself and the dapper gentleman, Cat greeted Lloyd, subdued. How much she had to learn! Yet she wondered if discourses on etiquette would include proprieties of giving a gentleman a piece of one's mind.

Lloyd, however, seemed so completely unaware of Cat's provocation that she began to doubt that he'd reported her to the hotel manager. Her own common sense told her that false accusations were always in poor taste, yet she didn't wish to let the matter drop. If he'd attempted to get her into trouble with the hotel management, she wanted to know. And if he were innocent, she wanted no suspicions between them.

As Cat considered how to make a delicate approach, Lloyd opened the subject for her.

"I should be quite perturbed with you, Miss Catherine."

"Whatever for?" she asked, truly stunned.

"For your insinuations yesterday evening. I'm really not totally dependent on my father, you know."

She shook her head prettily. "No, I didn't know, but I was rude to . . . to insinuate. You must understand, however, that I'm entirely self-dependent, and I must do as I see fit." She smiled then, quite pleased with herself for having told him so nicely to mind his own business.

"Well, Miss Catherine, do you see fit to seek

employment on a steamboat?" His tone of distaste irked her.

"There you go again!"

"What?"

"Sounding pompous!"

"I beg your pardon!"

"And now you're acting insulted when you've just insulted me!"

"Forgive me, Miss Catherine," Lloyd begged through a tortured smile, "but would you please lower your voice! People are staring."

"Let them," she said cheerfully, though embarrassment quickly scorched her. "I am, after all, an entertainer! And whether I choose to entertain nosy passersby here or an audience on a steamboat, it's entirely up to me."

Having so stated her position, Cat realized that the last thing she wanted to do was acquire the attentions of curious onlookers. She felt more than a little ashamed of her conduct, but, having gone thus far, she decided to confront Lloyd directly, electing, however, to lower her voice.

"I'm curious, Mr. Fairchild. Did your disapproval of my singing on the *Starlight* lead you to speak about it to the hotel manager?"

"Disapproval? Why, Miss Catherine! I delight in your voice, and I find you most alluring wherever you sing. My crime, I fear, is jealousy. I resent sharing you with so many admirers." With a courtly bow, Lloyd lifted her white-gloved hand to his lips.

Cat wasn't certain if Lloyd had just confessed or not, but the matter was forgotten when her eye was drawn toward a tall figure crossing the street. It was Raff Jordan and, holding his arm possessively, a tall, elegant young woman was keeping pace with his stride.

"Miss Catherine?" Puzzled, Lloyd followed her

gaze. "Ah, you've spied my sister, Augusta. Come; I'll introduce you."

Smoothly, Lloyd transferred Cat's hand to his arm, and she accepted his support gratefully. Her knees had begun to shake, and everything within her trembled. At the moment, she wished only to flee. Coming here had been a mistake, a terrible mistake, so unlike the scenes she'd envisioned, and there was little chance now of Raff's snatching her into his arms. Any love he avowed would be, not for her, but for Miss Augusta.

How beautiful she was! Even with a gaping mouth.

"My dress!" the woman exclaimed.

Cat felt her cheeks flame as Raff stared at her, scowling. No hint of recognition flickered from the clear blue eyes, but Miss Augusta's preoccupation with the white gown was another matter. Cat wished that Lloyd or Raff would say something, but Raff's look of disgust and Lloyd's bewilderment froze them both.

"Oh, did you have a dress similar to mine?" Cat asked, deliberately widening her already huge green eyes.

"I . . . I had one *exactly* like it—except for that ribboned collar."

"Then it wasn't exact, was it?" Lloyd said at last, as though his logic had resolved the predicament.

"But it was," Augusta insisted. "Don't you remember, Lloyd? Mama had it made for my commencement exercises."

"Does it matter?" Raff asked. He seemed to be bored.

"Of course it does! When one has a dress designed, one does not wish to think that another exists quite like it!" Augusta exclaimed.

"I wouldn't know," Raff admitted. Turning to Lloyd, he terminated the squabble. "You have us at a

115

disadvantage, sir, since you're the only one acquaint-
ed with your lovely companion.''

So he didn't recognize her! And he'd called her
"lovely"! Cat's heart fluttered with excitement as
Lloyd apologetically made the delayed introductions.

"Catherine Caldwell," Raff repeated, giving a low
bow.

His blue eyes traveled over her appreciatively,
boldly, and she felt her color deepen as he stared.
At least, she thought, *he finds me attractive!* And
how handsome he looked today with his tapered vest
and trim, light blue suit!

Their eyes caught, and Cat knew that this was the
moment she'd waited for. This was the expectant
hush. This was her cue to announce, "My friends call
me 'Cat'." But they were not alone, and so she said
nothing. The moment passed.

"So you entertain at the hotel by the Springs,"
Augusta Fairchild was saying now.

Breaking the magnetic hold of Raff's eyes, Cat
nodded, mute.

"Really, Raff darling, you must take me to hear
Miss Caldwell sing," Augusta said, conspicuously
tightening her hold on his arm.

"I'd like that," Raff answered, but his gaze remained on Cat. "Tonight, then?"

"Marvelous!" said Augusta.

Oh, no! thought Cat.

A spark of panic threatened to ignite her compo-
sure, but something in Raff's face—something smug,
something mocking—challenged her instead. So, he
wanted to hear her sing, did he? Well, sing she would,
and never would he see such a grand performance!

There was one problem, however, that Cat could
not overlook. Although Raff was obviously unobser-
vant, his companion had no such attribute. Augusta
Fairchild would surely recognize her discarded green

gown, and even more likely, she'd comment on Cat's wearing it!

Determined not to give the young woman that satisfaction, Cat excused herself, pleasantly saying, "I'll see you tonight! But now I really must return to my shopping."

Then, with Lloyd tagging along, Cat marched into the dry goods store and spent every penny she had on the rose-colored gown.

CHAPTER 11

"WHAT ON EARTH HAVE I DONE?" Cat asked herself again and again on the ride back to the hotel.

For days she'd exhausted herself with two jobs, and now she was penniless once more! She'd receive not a cent before the end of the month, still several days away, and with Mr. Smythe's ire already provoked, she dare not ask for an early pay.

It was all the doings of that Augusta Fairchild! Cat thought. Why couldn't that woman have kept her mouth shut? Wasn't it enough that she had Raff in her possessive grasp? And now, ironically, here was Cat herself, sitting beside the woman's brother!

At Lloyd's insistence, she'd sent the cook's helper ahead, and after a leisurely lunch and tour of Siloam Springs—also at Lloyd's insistence—Cat had consented to his persistent offer of dinner at the hotel.

She'd yet to dine there, preferring instead to eat in the kitchen with Archy or one of the other hotel workers, so the prospect of a fine meal, properly escorted, at an elegant table carried a certain appeal. She'd insisted, however, that the meal must be an early one, begging off with her need to rest before the evening's performance. But rest, in fact, was highly unlikely. It was Friday night, and there would be mountains of dishes to wash.

If only she'd told Raff the truth. . . . If only she'd identified herself to him. . . . If only she hadn't allowed that Augusta Fairchild to goad her into buying a dress she could not afford . . . ! Cat chided herself over and over as the buggy bounced back to the hotel.

"Penny for your thoughts," Lloyd said, breaking the rather lengthy silence.

Cat laughed. She'd almost told him, "It would be my only penny!" But she could hardly expect the son of a wealthy banker to understand.

Raff would have laughed at her foolishness, she knew. But she put her thoughts of him aside and tried to be charming to her present companion. It was easy actually. All she had to do was to steer Lloyd into conversations about himself.

At dinner, however, the menu provided more variety than their conversation, and Cat discovered delicacies she didn't know existed: *coquilles St. Jacques,* a baked scallop dish; *coq au vin,* a simmered blend of chicken, herbs and spices; Shrimp Creole with tomatoes and rice; and pheasant *en crème.* The simpler fare of filleted fish and sliced ham or beef, she'd sampled previously in Archy's kitchen, so she debated over which one of these exotic dishes to taste.

"What are you going to have?" she asked Lloyd. She could hardly ask him to recommend the hotel's best!

"We're dining so early, I think I'll have the heart of palm salad."

"Then so will I," Cat said, closing the large menu with a snap.

"The cuisine here is quite superb, don't you think?" Lloyd remarked, and when Cat responded with a nod, he said, "Someday I shall have to steal away the hotel's chef."

She didn't doubt that he could do it, but the casual comment left her vaguely disturbed.

The salad came, heaped on an enormous china plate, and seeing it, Cat exclaimed, "I cannot possibly finish this!" She had no idea that Archy served such generous portions, nor that his work was as eye-appealing as it was delectable. From now on, she'd have to pay more attention to his artistry. Perhaps he'd even allow her to experiment—if she could find the time. At the rate she'd spent her advanced wages, she'd be working two jobs forever!

True to her word, Cat pushed aside her meal with much remaining. Reluctantly, she joined Lloyd in the after-dinner coffee he'd ordered without asking her, but she insisted she must be going soon. As she thanked him for his invitations of the day, Augusta Fairchild entered the dining room with Raff close behind.

Cat's heart sank at the sight of the handsome couple. How well-suited they appeared, his tall, dark head contrasting with her majestically ornamented blond curls. And that gown! Cat had never seen anything like it with its cream-colored broché satin skirt and its black velvet bodice. Tiny cream, curled feathers traced the seams and hem of the skirt, encircling the ballooned sleeves and dipping up and down the revealing neckline. How grand Augusta looked as she glided toward them!

Cat's spirits plunged lower than the woman's black velvet neckline. As she gaped at Augusta, the answer to her earlier question became brutally clear. The rose-colored dress she had coveted and paid dearly to own was neither elegant nor grand—it was deservedly cheap!

"How nice to see you again, Miss Caldwell!" the young woman chimed pleasantly. "Do you mind if we join you?"

"Please do," Cat managed to answer, "but I must be leaving."

"She needs a bit of a rest before her performance," Lloyd explained.

Raff, who had given Cat only the barest greeting, asked her now, "Did you enjoy your salad, Miss Caldwell?"

"Oh, yes! It was most delicious," she said, avoiding his eyes.

"I'm glad you liked it," he went on. "It'd be a pity for that tree to die unappreciated."

"What!"

"See here, Jordan, sometimes you go too far." Lloyd placed a stilling hand on Cat who'd half-risen from her chair.

"Perhaps you go too far," Raff said coldly. Pointedly he stared at Lloyd's salad plate. Then, turning back to Cat, he spoke with more tolerance. "You might be interested to know, Miss Caldwell, that the main ingredient in your delectable salad is a cabbage-like bud that grows atop a palm. Generally the removal of that bud causes the death of the whole tree."

"I . . . I didn't know," Cat stammered.

"Don't apologize to him, dear," Augusta said with a toss of her feathered shoulder. "You'll only encourage him, and he's obsessed enough with some of his crazy notions."

To Cat's astonishment, she felt like hugging the woman, and mentally, she took back every unkind thought! Still, she felt confused by Raff's remarks. The thought of killing a tree for a partially eaten salad was too depressing.

Mumbling her excuses, Cat fled to her room, wishing fiercely that she could have that rest. But already she'd delayed too long, and Archy would be waiting. Her white dress dropped to the floor where she left it as she hurried into John's shirt and Pa's overalls and cap.

"Thought you might've run off," Archy said when she flew, breathless, into the cookhouse.

"Sorry I was late," she said as she surveyed the first round of dishes that the cook had thankfully left to soak.

"Whatcha got on your face?" Archy asked, curious. "Don't tell me some pretty little thing is already after you, boy."

Cat groaned. *Drat that rouge pot!* she thought, scrubbing her face clean. Good-naturedly, she endured the cook's teasing. Perhaps his mistaken conclusion would prove useful if he noticed that the kitchen boy's room stood often vacant.

"Archy," Cat asked after a while, "is it true that the bud used for a heart of palm salad kills the tree?"

"Reckon it does, but this here chicken's been axed, too."

More confused now, Cat was sorry she'd asked, and after that she plied the head cook with questions about his culinary arts, glad that he was in an unusually talkative mood. The interesting conversation kept her mind off Raff.

She wasn't surprised, however, when he appeared, stopping by to say hello. Since the last batch of pans lay soaking, she sincerely hoped Raff wouldn't stay long.

"I just wanted to see how you're doing," he told her.

"Fine."

"Anything you need?"

"No."

"Work going all right?"

"Fine."

"You're not very talkative tonight, are you?"

She shook her head, and there was silence. Raff still made no move to leave. If he didn't soon, she'd be late for her performance, too!

"You here by yourself?" Cat asked, hoping her reminder would nudge Raff toward the door.

"At the moment, yes."

"Oh."

"Cat, is something wrong?"

"No."

Raff sighed. "Did you see the *Starlight?* It's docked at the Springs."

"I saw."

"Would you like to go with me and say hello to the captain?"

"No!"

"Suit yourself," he said, bidding her an abrupt good night.

Even though Raff had taken the path to the docks, she allowed sufficient time to be sure she'd not bump into him on the hotel's covered walk. Then she hastened to her room, wondering how she would ever get ready.

Before the door had closed well behind her, she'd unfastened the straps on the bib overalls and whisked off her stocking cap. Heading toward the wardrobe, she stepped out of her moccasins, leaving a trail of clothing across the room. With one hand she yanked the pins from her hair, and with the other, she lifted her rose dress from its hook and shook out the wrinkles. Then she slipped it over her head.

The color and fit were becoming, but Cat scarcely gave herself a glance in the mirror. On the bed behind her, a package of some sort was reflected in the glass, and she wheeled around to see what it was. A note atop informed her that one of the maids had let herself into the room to deposit a collection of hand-me-down gowns for her costume wardrobe.

When she'd scanned the message, Cat let out a cry. She'd spent all of her money for nothing! Even Augusta Fairchild could not possibly recognize these clothes!

Having not a minute to spare, Cat didn't bother to try on any of the gowns for tonight's performance. Yet she knew at least one would be a perfect fit. Ma

Tate had told her that God would provide what she needed to use the gifts He'd given. And tonight she'd needed a gown.

"I don't even know how to trust You, God! Help me," she cried.

The knock on the door startled her. "Who is it?"

"Raff Jordan, Miss Caldwell. May I speak to you, please?"

"J—just a moment."

Quickly she ran a brush through her hair, which had fallen loosely about her shoulders, and when she'd dabbed fresh color on her lips and cheeks, she kicked the kitchen boy's clothing beneath the bed. Cautiously, she opened the door only a crack, fearful that she'd overlooked some telling item in her haste.

"I came to apologize," Raff said. "Fairchild's right—sometimes I go too far."

"I assure you, Mr. Jordan, I'm not in the habit of killing whole trees for one tasty morsel." In light of his apology, Cat felt she owed him that much.

Raff rewarded her with a half-smile. "It's not always that way. Sometimes the trees live; sometimes the trunks are used for pilings. It's heedless slaughter for faddish tastes that I abhor."

"I can understand that," she told him, "and your apology is accepted, Mr. Jordan. Now, if you'll excuse me, I must complete my toilette."

With a low bow, Raff assured her he'd be waiting.

As soon as she'd closed the door, Cat hurried back to her hairdressing. Practiced now, she swept the flowing tresses into a high twist, leaving saucy ringlets to dangle about her face. When she'd satisfied herself with the results, she slipped the pink-plumed aigrette into place atop her chestnut hair. Inexpensively dressed or not, the girl in the mirrored glass looked charming.

Wearing her white gloves to hide her reddened hands, Cat opened the door of her room and found Raff leaning lazily against the flocked paper on the

124

corridor wall. His first glance reflected delight in her appearance, but as his blue eyes traveled upward, the expression changed. A scowl darkened his face like a sudden thunder cloud, and he lurched forward, yanking the aigrette from her hair.

The pink plumes crushed under Raff's dress boots as Cat shrieked at him.

"What do you think you're doing?"

"I . . ." He stopped then, his red angered face going white with shock. "I don't know."

Looking thoroughly ashamed of himself, Raff bent to pick up the dangling, limp feathers that Cat snatched out of his hand.

"It was once a flamingo," he said as though he'd just pronounced last rites.

"It was once my hat!" Cat retorted, unable to hold back her tears. "And I didn't see you ripping the feathers off Miss Fairchild's gown! There'd be precious little left if you did!"

She slammed the door in his face then, but not before she'd seen the flicker of a smile.

Oh, that man infuriated her! It was bad enough that he made her feel like a murderess, but now he'd ruined her costume! And her hair, tumbling down, would have to be redone.

When he rapped again on the door, Cat barked, "Go away! And take your apologies with you!"

"No apologies here, Missy!" Mr. Smythe's voice thundered back. "You've got five minutes to get on that stage, or you'll be the one going." Without waiting for her excuses, the manager clomped down the hall.

Shaken, Cat dried her eyes with a gloved finger then jerked the pins from her hair. She raked the brush through, unflinching, until her hair, fluffed and flowing, shone in the lamplight. A vulnerable little girl stared back, wide-eyed, from the mirror.

"God, help that child," she said.

Something within calmed then, and she began to see

the humor of the awful, aching, ridiculous day. By the time she reached the small platform of a stage, a quick glance at Raff's face told her that she felt more composed than he. He stared at her oddly—wistfully?—and that poignant look moved her to flash him a forgiving smile. He winced, and she looked away.

The Fairchilds had returned, Cat saw, acknowledging their presence with a smiling nod, and in a corner, Mr. Smythe stood with arms folded and legs apart as if waiting to toss her on her ear. Mischievously she beamed at him, then flounced across the stage.

Cat recognized some of the audience, and their welcoming applause warmed her before she'd begun to sing. But the faces fell away as the songs came forth, lively and fun, tender and sad, filled with the sweet harmony of girlish charm and womanly desires. Skillfully she swayed the audience from merriment to tears until even Mr. Smythe responded.

"Bravo!" Lloyd shouted, jumping to his feet at her final curtsy.

Impulsively she blew him a kiss before showering the whole room. When she saw Raff's sharp glance, she wondered: Could he be jealous? Impossible! she told herself, especially when he had the luscious Miss Augusta fawning at his side.

"You do have a lovely voice," the woman said when Cat, at Lloyd's insistence, joined them. "With your hair down like that, you look to be no older than fourteen! Doesn't she, Raff darling?"

"Raff darling" chose that precise moment to cough.

Cat ignored him. "I've been told that before, Miss Fairchild. But would you tell me something? I'm curious—what kind of feathers are those which grace your lovely gown?"

"Why, I'm not sure. Raff, do you know?"

But choking now, Raff excused himself from the room. When he returned moments later, his dinner partner was asking Cat about her locket.

"I couldn't help noticing it, Miss Caldwell. It's quite exquisite. Have you had it appraised?"

"Appraised?"

"To determine its value. Aren't you interested in its monetary worth?"

"Not in the least."

"Some things aren't valued in terms of money, Augusta," Raff said. "Isn't that right, Miss Caldwell?"

"If you say so," she answered, not wishing to give him the satisfaction of her agreement.

Augusta, however, took Cat's response as one of encouragement. "Do have the locket appraised, Miss Caldwell. If we can come to terms, I'd be most happy to purchase it from you."

"You and your antique jewelry," Lloyd said, disgusted with his sister's persistent discussion. "The only reason you want the old thing is because Miss Catherine has it."

"Don't be so infantile!" Augusta snapped. "Now, see what you've done! You've insulted Miss Caldwell—calling her lovely antique locket an 'old thing.' She'll think you're trying to bring down the price."

"I'm sorry if I've misled you, Miss Fairchild, but there is no price," Cat said, clutching the locket against her. "This belonged to my mother and her mother before that. And to me anyway, the locket is priceless."

"There!" Lloyd slapped the small table. "That settles the matter."

"Oh, do be quiet!" Augusta scolded. "If you change your mind, Miss Caldwell, you will let me know."

"Of course," Cat assured her without any intentions of ever doing so. "Now, if you will excuse me, I really must retire."

"Don't go, Miss Catherine!" Lloyd begged. "It is still early."

"Not for me."

"You said that last night, but we had a good time, didn't we?"

A movement from Raff brought his scowling face into focus. Puzzled, Cat wondered why he was so easily irked by his prospective brother-in-law. Lloyd could be annoying, but what was it to Raff?

"I had a pleasant time, Lloyd," Cat agreed reluctantly, "but it is very late, and tonight I'm truly exhausted."

"If I press you now, everyone will think me a cad," Lloyd said peevishly.

"Perhaps they'd be right," Raff commented dryly.

Lloyd squirmed under his hostile stare. "All right! We'll say good night for now, Miss Catherine, but I'll expect you to make amends for the loss of a promising evening. Sunday afternoon perhaps? We could row across the Springs."

"Oh! I'd love to view them closely!" Cat voiced her thoughts without realizing she'd given consent.

"Splendid!" Lloyd said, and she was too tired to argue. Lloyd's company was not that objectionable, and she did want to see the Springs.

She would have preferred Raff's company, of course, but even without Augusta Fairchild to entice him, he'd expressed nothing but censure and distaste. No wonder! Everything she'd done was wrong! The salad she'd innocently ordered was embarrassing enough. But, worse, Cat hadn't taken off her gloves to eat it! No lady would make such a mistake, commit such a breach of etiquette. But then, no lady would have such red hands!

CHAPTER 12

BESIDES THE CHRONIC FATIGUE and the constant threat of being caught, Cat's double roles at the hotel kept her from making friends. She'd asked the maid not to do her room, afraid the girl would spot her dual wardrobe, and the gesture succeeded in winning attentions she preferred to keep at bay. Little courtesies were offered, which Cat found difficult to resist, and only need and lack of funds forced her to ask to borrow needle, scissors, and spools of thread.

The young maid's bobbing about the room made Cat ache for a friend with whom she could encourage pleasant chatter. How she wished the Tate family were close enough for brief visits between chores—hers or theirs. But seldom did Cat have more than an hour or two between the mountains of pots and pans, and after she left the lounge at night, she fell into bed, still exhausted at daybreak.

Today, however, the Saturday breakfast crowd had been slack, and she found herself with two full hours before the noon meal. She hoped now she could remember the simple stitching Ma Tate had shown her, for she had three elegant gowns for additional costumes and one dress, a fashionable dotted Swiss, to use for everyday wear. The latter had been left behind by a guest, who'd presumably made a hasty departure, and, when she'd proven untraceable, the maid had brought the dress to Cat.

"Lawsy, Miss Catherine, you can't pin these here dresses yourself," the young girl scolded, for that was exactly what Cat had been attempting to do.

Knowing the maid was right, Cat sighed, "I suppose I could use some help."

One sleeveless gown required tucks in the brown velvet bodice and a shortened hem on the brown lace-paneled skirt front, but the bustle and train were best left alone, as the girls decided, giggling. Another gown, this one of Nile green China crepe, fell so low on the squared corsage that near-hysteria erupted until the maid had pinned the shirred gauze, which draped the shoulders. An epaulet of pink blossoms needed repositioning, but the corselet remained intact, bound lightly by a sash of black watered satin.

Fortunately the departed hotel guest proved slender, so the ruffled bodice and banded waist of the pale blue Swiss muslin fit Cat perfectly, as did the balloon, ruffled sleeves. Shortening the dress was a simple matter of removing the lowest of six ruffles that encircled the fashionably trim skirts. Cat felt heartened. She could do that easily!

One of the garments handed down for a costume, an elaborate Parisian toilette of black silk, seemed tailor-made for her, and both girls clapped their hands in delight. The dress would have been impossible otherwise! From the full round skirt a draped tablier bordered each side with double rows of pleated pink crepon. The shell-pleating also trimmed the collar, the cuffs of the long-sleeves, and even the armholes with another row of the pink crepon flouncing the skirt above the shoe.

"Would you look at that!" the maid exclaimed. "Same as if it was made for you."

"I expect it was, in a way," Cat said, smiling at the picture-perfect reflection in her mirror. So this was the dress God had provided for her to wear last night! Old-fashioned though it was, the gown was obviously once quite costly. But, no doubt, its original owner had not needed to spend her last cent!

Neither did I, Cat thought, sighing. She wondered just how long it would be before she'd really learn to trust God—or anybody else for that matter! Raff had teased her, saying in the kitchen that she'd begun to trust him. And she had. She did. But not when it concerned herself. Not when Augusta Fairchild hung onto his arm!

No, she realized, that wasn't fair. Raff had provided her with food, shelter, and transportation, even when she was a stranger to him. He'd arranged a home, a place for her to stay, with the Tates, and no one could have chosen a more loving, gracious family. Even now he showed his concern, visiting her at the sink whenever he could. He cared; he wanted only what was best for Cat. If only Catherine could say the same!

By Sunday afternoon, Cat had tucked the brown velvet gown, which thankfully hid her clumsy stitching, and she'd ripped the bottom ruffle from the pale blue dotted Swiss. At the maid's insistence—and at the admission of her own inexperienced hand—she'd gratefully accepted the girl's assistance on the China crepe. To Cat's astonishment, the girl had reversed her appreciative words.

"Don't be thankin' me, Miss Catherine. I'd of give my eye teeth to work on soft, purty material like this gown."

"But you've done so much already," Cat protested.

"No'm." The girl shook her plump face. "You've

been the giver—with them purty songs and the way you clean your own room. You treat me nice, Miss Catherine—like I was a real person, a lady or somethin'."

"Why, you are!" Cat exclaimed.

"Not many folks would be agreein'," the maid chuckled, unabashed.

When the girl left with the Nile green gown, Cat stared after her, wondering. Was appreciation another form of trust? And did receiving require more trust than giving? When she thought once more of God as giver, the thought troubled her. He'd provided her with costume, as Ma Tate had said He would, to use her singing talent that He had also given. But even though those gifts were a delight, she'd been slow to receive them, slow to trust.

What of the gifts she hadn't wanted—the loneliness, the struggles, the hard times, the circumstances she'd just as soon have done without? What good, what delight, had come from those?

As she sought the answer, a glimpse of truth came. The unpleasant gifts had prepared her for those that she'd enjoy. If she'd been unaccustomed to a lonely, difficult life, she certainly wouldn't be seizing upon her opportunities now. She wouldn't have traveled or sung in a hotel or met the Tates. She wouldn't even know Raff existed!

She saw him midafternoon as she stepped into the rowboat Lloyd had rented for their tour across the Springs. He was coming out of the hotel with a package under his arm and an increasingly constant scowl upon his face. Beneath the covered walk to the kitchen house, Raff had not spied her, and idly Cat wondered which of her two persons he'd come to see.

When he entered the small building, Cat squinted, hoping for another glimpse as he came out, but Lloyd had turned the boat away, placing her back to the hotel and grounds. Unable to resist another look, she tilted her chin toward the shore.

"That sun is too bright for delicate skin, Miss Catherine," Lloyd said, reminding her of his presence. "I wish you'd brought your parasol."

"What? Oh." Abruptly, Cat turned back to her companion, causing the rowboat to rock slightly. She placed a steadying hand on each side, thinking how unlike a raft this was. Now what had Lloyd been saying?

"Do you think we should go back for it?" he asked, and at her blank look, added, "Your parasol."

"I don't have one," she blurted truthfully.

The oars stopped midair. "You don't have a parasol?" Lloyd was aghast. "But all ladies have parasols."

"I see. Then since I'm without one, that must mean I'm no lady," Cat snapped. Raff wouldn't have cared if she'd had one or not, she realized, but Lloyd suffered so under poor appearances. Perhaps he was one of those people to whom the maid referred, pompous in their treatment of those of inferior station. Regardless Lloyd most definitely would never be one to rip pink plumes from a lady's head and stomp them on the ground! Not even if he'd held strong preservationist beliefs.

The thought, however, made a funny picture, and so did the speechless shock registering on Lloyd's face now. Cat took pity on him and on his stifled ways.

"There's a lovely pink parasol I plan to purchase next week," she admitted, "but at the moment, sir, you've caught me at a disadvantage. To obtain passage to Florida, I had to travel light."

Whether or not her explanation made sense, Lloyd snatched upon it with immense relief. He pressed her no further, nor did he suggest they terminate their outing to protect Cat from the glaring sun.

Twenty yards or so from shore, Lloyd pulled in the oars.

"There are several springs in this stretch of the river, but this one is my favorite. Wait until the ripples settle, Miss Catherine, and you'll be able to see."

Cat did as bidden, and when the disturbed waters rested again, she gave a little gasp.

"It's like a fairy's cave!" she exclaimed, and indeed it was.

Archways of many colors had been cut by the pulsating water that gushed from the mouth of the spring, and the patient river had shaped and smoothed the crusted stone. Deep crevices plunged at irregular angles, and the sun, slanting in the western sky, bathed this architectural wonder with golden light.

"Wouldn't it be wonderful to slip inside?" Cat said wistfully.

"It's exhilarating!"

"You've been down there?"

Lloyd chuckled. "I see I've impressed you at last, Miss Catherine. Yes, I've taken a swim or two."

"Tell me! What's it like?"

"Too beautiful to describe. On a cloudy day, the colors change from the yellow-gold you see now to a blue-green wonder. But the fun of it is shooting up with the force of the spring. It's like being weightless."

"Oh, I can't imagine," Cat admitted, though she tried. With eager curiosity, she leaned over the water, peering down.

"Careful," Lloyd cautioned, and as he did, the boat tipped unsteadily. "Here, Miss Catherine. Let me hold you so you can have a better look."

Giving her no opportunity to object, Lloyd clasped her tiny waist. Cat stiffened against his unwelcomed touch, settling herself back onto her seat. How would a lady ask a gentleman to remove his hands? she wondered, when he made no such effort. Flustered by her awkward position, Cat turned toward him to speak, and, doing so, she placed herself squarely in Lloyd's arms.

In a flash, his lips came down upon hers, and his hold tightened. Struggling, she tried to pull away, but the lurching movement of the boat dissuaded her. She'd like to see the spring cavern underwater, but not in a dotted Swiss gown!

"Lloyd, please!" she gasped.

"Catherine, Catherine," he whispered huskily. "Don't you feel anything for me?"

"Frankly, no," she said because it was true. His head shot up, pouting. "Oh, don't look so pathetic, Lloyd. I'm disappointed, too. That was, after all, my first kiss."

"Really, Miss Catherine?" The thought seemed to encourage him. "Perhaps another. . . ."

"No!" She leaned back as far as she dared. "Take me ashore, Lloyd. I fear I've had too much sun." And probably, she thought, too much Lloyd.

Amazingly he complied, and Cat wondered if it were because he'd been offended or because he did not wish to be held responsible for a lady's crisped skin. Either way, his steady rowing served her purpose, getting safely back to her room.

Once there, Cat stretched out on the crocheted coverlet on her bed, dreamily recalling the fairy cavern sculpted in the rocks beneath the river. How she wished she could explore the dancing lights and dark crevices with the airy abandonment of those silvery fish that darted in and out. Magnified by the clearness of the water, the lovely scene appeared to be at surface's edge, and Cat had longed to touch it. But reaching out had tipped the boat.

"No, it didn't!" Cat sat up abruptly. "Oh, that Lloyd!" He'd teetered the boat by advancing from his seat to hers! And she'd thought he'd come, a gentleman, to the rescue.

Vexed with his behavior and her own naïveté, Cat answered the rap at the door churlishly. Raff's blue eyes, wide but amused, did nothing to help her disposition.

"What do you want?" she asked ungraciously.

"To see you, m'lady," he said with a low bow, mocking.

"Well, now you've seen me. Good-by."

"Catherine, wait!" His large hand stopped the door's latching. "I've come bearing gifts and apologies for my boorish manners, so don't shut me out. Go for a walk with me."

She eyed him suspiciously.

"Please, Miss Caldwell."

Cat sighed. Then taking the arm he offered, she strolled with him, out of the hotel and around the lush grounds.

Whatever Raff had wanted apparently could wait, for he made no move to apologize or even to speak, and the package he'd brought swung lightly from his free hand. His other arm pinioned hers against him, making her painfully aware of his nearness, of the rise and fall of his breath.

She wondered at the languor flowing through her, cleansing her of annoyance and suspicions, and bathing her with a curious delight. The very touch of her hand upon his sleeve sent prickles racing, pulsating like the gush of a bursting spring, and she felt weightless.

"Would you like to sit down?" Raff asked, and she nodded, afraid to trust her voice.

His broad hand slipped around her waist as he guided her to a slatted wooden bench that was set beside tall azaleas beneath a live oak tree. In this secluded spot, no tourists ventured at the moment, and only the trill of a mockingbird and the chatter of squirrels broke the silence.

Raff placed his package on the far edge of the bench

136

before settling himself beside her. He opened his mouth to speak, but confusion flickered across his face as his eyes caught hers. What had he seen? Cat wondered. Her dark lashes lowered, veiling the depth of her emotions, but a slight tremor betrayed her, and he took her in his arms.

His lips brushed her forehead; his warm breath teased the flush of her cheeks, and when she thought she could stand it no longer, she tilted back her head until his mouth rested softly upon hers. These were not Lloyd's lips felt with cool, analytical detachment. This was not Lloyd's name that escaped her lips.

Raff's kiss silenced her. His hand pressed hard against the nape of her neck, and she yielded to his embrace, meeting it with an intensity of her own. Her arms crept about his broad shoulders, shyly at first, then more boldly. How long had she waited to hold him like this, to be held?

Despite the day's humidity, when he pulled away, Cat felt a sudden chill. His hands unclasped hers from around his neck, and she yanked them away, hugging herself, steeling herself against the cold blue stare that slowly iced his face.

"Do you make a habit of kissing strangers?" he cruelly asked.

The words of revulsion dealt her a swift blow, and as she reeled from it, her mindless arm arced upward in desperate defense. Denial screamed from every fiber of her being, urging her to hurt him, to retaliate, to stop another single threatening word. She slapped his face hard.

Staggering from the bench, she fled down the path to the hotel—a wounded bird in flight, broken and blinded by tears. Somehow she stumbled into her room, unattended, where she flung herself headlong across the bed. Her body, racked with sobs and shame, ached incredibly until she thought she'd die.

But feeling too luckless for death, it slowly occurred to her that the throbbing in her arm was quite real.

Curiosity dragged her attention to her hand that strained against the soiled white glove. One by one, she slipped her fingers out of their silken confinement, staring in disbelief at the purple swells that raged about each knuckle. She had not slapped Raff at all, she realized. Instead, her doubled fist had socked him squarely in the jaw!

CHAPTER 13

"HE DESERVED IT!" Cat told herself. But she supposed that she deserved the rapidly swelling hand. Never having hit anyone before, she could only speculate on the condition of Raff's jaw. She sincerely hoped that she'd blackened neither of those cherished eyes. What would he think of her now!

Only what he'd always thought of Catherine Caldwell—that the woman was no lady. Why else would he treat her with such contempt? She certainly hadn't seen him ripping feathers from Augusta Fairchild's bodice or mocking her choice of cuisine. And, if he kissed her in the hotel gardens, Miss Fairchild would surely have no cause to slap his face!

Cat winced. A lady might slap; she'd never sock with a fist.

Furious with herself, Cat scoffed at her disheveled person in front of the mirror.

"Imposter! That's what you are. Not a kitchen boy. Not a lady. Pretending! That's all you've been doing, and it's got to stop!"

But how?

Either way, Raff didn't want her, except perhaps to take advantage. How malevolent his kiss seemed now! A condescending touch for one of an inferior station. His treatment seemed so dreadful and so clear that the knowledge pained her far more than her battered hand.

He'd kissed her because he'd supposed, correctly, that he could—nothing more. And she'd allowed him to—actually asked for it. For one splendid moment, she'd believed he felt something real, but the pretense, again, was hers. How foolish she felt now! How ashamed and betrayed by her own emotions.

She wished she could undo the damage she'd caused herself and Raff, damage not only from her puny blow, but from her deceptions. But it was too late. Raff thought the worse of her, and nothing she could say would improve the matter. If it weren't so sad, it'd be funny, she thought. Funny that he'd cultivated her trust, Cat's trust, when she, all the while, was deceiving him!

"Oh, dear God!" she sobbed, rubbing her purpled hand. "I never meant for any of this to happen!"

Creeping back to the crocheted spread, she sank in despair. What havoc she'd created, hurting the one person she most loved! And she did love him, she realized. Having no criteria by which to gauge, it'd taken awhile for her to admit it to herself—to be aware of it herself—and now that she had, what good did it do?

"No more pretenses," she said, giving the mattress a determined thump. At least she could be honest with herself, she thought. Still it wasn't easy. Unless she could convince herself that she didn't care, it'd be impossible to stay at the Springs, to be so vulnerable, to chance Raff's casual kitchen visits.

But she did care; she did love him. And after so many weeks together on the river, she and Raff were no strangers. Even if the scorned singer disappeared from his life, what hope was there for a deeper relationship with a kitchen boy? She'd miss that friendship with him, but both of her would have to go!

Once she'd made up her mind to get away from Raff, as far away as she could, Cat puzzled over the financial status that bound her. If she left now, she'd forfeit her hard-earned wages in both jobs. Yet, if she delayed much longer, the *Starlight* would be gone.

Since she had no idea when the captain planned on leaving, Cat determined to find out. She dared not set foot on the steamboat again as Catherine Caldwell because of Mr. Smythe's all-seeing eyes, but the kitchen boy's job had not been threatened. It was almost time to don Pa's clothes anyway, so she did so now, then tugged the thick stocking cap over her ears with distaste.

"Oh, I hate this thing!" she complained to her reflection.

The heavy knit, which she'd welcomed during the bitter winter, plastered her hair against a perspiring head now that the weather had warmed. Thankfully, she'd be rid of it soon.

Fully attired, Cat opened the door a crack, and quickly shut it. In the corridor, Raff paced, the package once again in his hand.

"What a bother this is!" she mumbled to herself. Since she couldn't allow Raff to see her coming out of Catherine Caldwell's room, she slipped quietly out the window.

As soon as she'd done so, she wondered what difference it would make. Raff would find out soon enough that she'd tricked him, especially when both of her were gone at once! Still, she couldn't bear confronting his displeasure, nor did she want her last memory of him to be his pained, shocked expression when she'd belted him across the jaw.

She wished she could have glimpsed his face just now in the hall, but his back had been turned so she could not survey the damage. It surprised her that he was still at the hotel, and she wondered if he'd stay for the night's performance. She sincerely hoped not!

What she did hope was that she could see him once more as his friend, as the person he knew best, as the boy for whom he'd shown such deep concern. If she could, she'd tell him good-by. If she could not, she'd at least have the memory of ending their friendship on a pleasant note.

Standing on tiptoe behind a partial screen of shrub, Cat yanked shut the window to her hotel room. Then, crouching low, she sneaked through the bushes.

A pair of hands reached through and snatched her out.

"Singing lessons, huh?" Mr. Smythe bellowed. "I warned you, boy, I'd be keeping an eye on you."

Cat's heart pounded in her throat. "It's not the way it looks, Mr. Smythe."

"Boy, I reckon you'd say most anything to miss out on that thrashing I promised, now wouldn't you?"

"No! I . . . I wouldn't!" she protested as the hotel manager dragged her along by the seat of her pants. "Mr. Smythe, please! If you'll just go to . . . to Miss Caldwell's room, you'll see. Honest," she said, hoping against hope that Raff would still be in the hall.

With a snort, the manager altered his direction, heading—to Cat's immense relief—toward the side door nearest her room. The slamming of the door, the shuffling of half-dragged feet, and the stomping of Mr. Smythe's boots caught Raff's immediate attention.

"What's going on here?" he demanded as the manager cut toward him, jerking Cat in his wake.

"Just a little hotel business," Mr. Smythe answered curtly. His sausagelike fist pounded heavily on the bedroom door.

"If you're looking for Miss Caldwell," Raff offered mildly, "I don't believe she's in."

"Hmmpf. We'll see about that," the manager

142

snapped. Then taking his keys from a pocket, he fumbled for one, which he slipped unnecessarily into the lock. The knob turned readily beneath his hand— it would have without the key, since Cat, having unbolted it from the inside, had had no opportunity to secure it from outside.

"She's gone!"

"I . . . I was try . . . trying to tell you that, Mr. Smythe."

"Then 'spose you tell me quick why you were sneaking out that window!" Violently, he jerked her into the room.

Cat gasped for breath. "I . . ."

"Let the boy go, Smythe." Raff stepped in behind, and laid his package on the rumpled crocheted spread. Thus freed, his hands cupped against his narrow hips. "I can't say exactly what's transpired here, but if you're suggesting the . . . the boy . . . is having a clandestine affair with Miss Caldwell, I think that's absurd!"

"Do you now?" the manager sneered. "And what business is it of yours?"

"A lot," Raff answered. "The boy's been in my care for some time, and I vouch for him."

Cat felt the blue eyes on her, but until now she'd avoided his stare. Wriggling under Mr. Smythe's slackening grasp, she turned to her rescuer with an appreciative smile, but she bit her lip in despair when she glimpsed the ugly red welt high on Raff's cheek-bone.

"Well, I don't know," the manager said, hesitantly. "I told this boy to stay away from here, or I'd give him a thrashing he wouldn't forget."

"That, sir, would be most unwise of you," Raff warned. He stepped closer, his voice menacing, his towering height a threat. Suddenly he laughed. "I think you'll agree, Mr. Smythe, that the boy here is too young," he stressed the words, "for anything illicit. If improprieties have occurred, no doubt Miss Caldwell is at fault. Perhaps you should thrash her instead for being so seductive.''

Cat's mouth dropped, and with a determined twist, she freed herself from the manager's grip.

"Catherine Caldwell is not that kind of girl! She's . . . she's nice!" Even *she* couldn't call herself a lady!

Raff rubbed the angry mark on his cheek. "Is that so?" he said, his face and tone expressionless. But his eyes hinted amusement. "Then, were she here, I'd beg for her pardon."

Cat glared at him until the manager's voice regained her attention.

"The Caldwell woman isn't my problem. This boy is for not minding what I say!" At Smythe's move toward Cat, Raff quietly placed himself between. "All right! I won't lay a hand on him, but I'm not going to have him hanging around here any more. You're fired, boy! Now, get your things and clear out."

"But . . . but my wages!"

"You should've thought of that sooner."

"You have every right to fire whom you please," Raff admitted grudgingly, "but none to withhold what's due."

The manager's jaw clamped tightly. "I've had my say, and the boy's to clear out," he repeated stubbornly. "No one gets paid here until the end of the month. If he comes back then, he'll be paid for working days—not a penny more!"

"Fair enough," Raff said, totally unaware that he'd just given away the paltry sum for which she'd worked so hard.

Shooing them out of the bedroom, the manager locked the door and marched away with a last word to Cat. "Clear out, and I better not catch you around here until payday."

Cat made a face against his back, and Raff, noticing, chuckled.

"What'll you do now?" he asked softly.

She shrugged. "I'll manage."

"I'm very aware that you're independent, Cat," he snapped, suddenly angry, "bbt if I hadn't been here just now, you'd be tending a very sore behind!"

"I know." She shuddered. "Thanks."

"Thanks," he mocked. "I thought we were friends."

"We are!"

"Then tell me what you're going to do."

"It's not that simple, Raff."

"Make it simple! Try trusting me for a change!"

"I do!" She flung her hands out, exasperated.

Catching sight of the purple swells, Raff winced. Then seizing her wrist, he pulled her toward him, beginning a none-too-gentle probe.

"That hurts!" she complained, trying to snatch her fingers from the pressure of his broad thumb.

"Oh, be still!" he commanded before letting go. "Nothing is broken—at least nothing I can see," he stated sarcastically. "I don't suppose you'll tell me how that happened?"

"What difference does it make?"

"A lot."

She couldn't tell him; she just couldn't!

"I hurt myself," she said at last. "Nobody else did it, if that's what you're thinking."

With his head tilted back, Raff's slitted eyes swept her with disdain. "Really? I don't recall your being so clumsy."

"Well, maybe I am!" she shouted at him. "Maybe I'm very clumsy where people are concerned. Maybe I get myself into situations which catch me completely off-guard. But you can be sure of one thing, Raff Jordan. I seldom make the same mistake twice."

"Easy, Cat." He placed a stilling hand on her shoulder, and guided her toward the outer door.

"Let's keep this conversation to ourselves, shall we?"

His calm voice angered her more. "I suppose *you're* afraid of a public scene, too!" she said, thinking of Lloyd.

"I don't know what you mean!" Raff said, his volume excelling hers. "I am merely trying to shield you from enraging Mr. Smythe—even though you probably do deserve that thrashing!"

"Oh." Why must he always make her feel so foolish?

Meekly, she followed him outside. "I . . . I guess it wouldn't hurt to tell you what I plan to do."

"I guess not," he answered dryly.

"The captain of the *Starlight* promised me a job if I should ever want it."

"And do you?"

"Oh, yes! It's something I've thought about often, but I kept putting it off. Now I've no excuse."

"I see." His tone suggested little enthusiasm.

"It's what I want to do," she said defiantly, trying to convince him—and herself.

Raff sounded annoyed. "Then do it!" Suddenly he sighed. "Come on. I'll go with you."

"Where?"

"To see the captain."

"No! I mean . . . that's not necessary."

"Perhaps not, but I insist." His firmness stilled her arguments, but when they reached the dock, she tried again.

"Really, Raff. I can handle this myself!"

"I'm sure you can," he said. Yet he hauled her on board the *Starlight* where he immediately ignored her as he inquired for the captain.

Cat squirmed in the gathering dusk. This was not what she had planned at all! Dressed in her boyish attire, she'd simply hoped to gain information about the steamboat's departure. If luck were with her, she might even be able to finish the month out, singing at the hotel, before the *Starlight* left the Springs, thereby collecting her wages from both jobs. The captain's cheery remarks, however, killed all hopes of such good fortune.

"Aye, we'll depart here by tomorrow noon."

"Tomorrow?" she asked pathetically, and Raff gave her a sharp look.

"Does that interfere with your busy schedule?" he jeered.

Mutely she shook her head, thinking of her wages sinking down the drain.

Quizzically the captain glanced from one face to the other. "What's this? Another passenger for the *Starlight?*" he asked amiably.

"No, sir," Raff clarified, "we've come regarding the matter of a promised . . ."

"Captain!" Cat interrupted. Behind Raff's back, she signaled the older man, who appeared increasingly perplexed. "May I speak with you? *Alone*, sir?"

Disgruntled Raff stepped aside at the captain's assent, and when Cat left him, he stood leaning over the railing, his expression blacker than the darkening water. She hoped he'd be there when she returned from her private chat, and she cast him an expectant look that fell from his unyielding profile. He was angry with her, but that couldn't be helped. If she'd allowed him to continue, she'd be scrubbing pots in the galley!

Having followed the captain up two narrow flights of stairs and into a cubicle, she accepted his permission to be seated.

"Now, lad," he said, not unkindly, "will you tell me what this is about?"

Not knowing where to start, Cat whisked off her stocking cap, and the hair, which she'd pinned lightly, fell about her shoulders.

"I'd like to sing for your passengers, sir, if you'll still have me."

The captain's eyes widened, then seized with the joke, he laughed heartily, slapping his knee.

"Miss Caldwell, isn't it? Well, lad or lass, I thought you looked familiar," he admitted, still chuckling. "Oh! And your Mr. Jordan doesn't know!" Apparently that knowledge amused him even more. "And to think!" he gasped for breath between the waves of laughter. "You two were traveling companions!"

The hilarity was infectious, and Cat joined in. "It is ridiculous, isn't it?" she said as soon as she was able.

"Oh, my." The captain wiped his eyes. "I don't know when I've had such a good laugh."

"Nor I," Cat agreed.

But in moments, the two had entered a discussion of the unhumorous situations that had led Cat to her present dilemma.

"You'll have me crying soon!" He sniffed. "My dear Catherine—I must call you that since you remind me of my own granddaughter—I wish I could help you out with that Mr. Smythe and your wages, but, alas, the man has his own grudges against me."

"Please, sir, I didn't mean to burden you with my problem. I was merely stating facts."

"I realize that, but there's something defenseless about you, Catherine, despite your high spirit, and it makes a man want to protect you, I suppose. Now, now! Wipe that frown away." Standing abruptly, the captain held out his hand. "Welcome aboard the *Starlight*."

"Then I have the job!"

"Of course, my dear. I'm a man of my word, and I'm glad to have you."

Unable to suppress her joy, Cat gave a squeal of delight. Then, hair in place, she descended the stairs to the lower deck, promising the captain she'd be ready for the morrow's departure. He accompanied her, however, to the deck where Raff paced impatiently in and out of the torchlight.

"All's well, Mr. Jordan," the captain said with a farewell gesture. "The promised job is secure, and you've no cause to worry about the . . . the lad." Then with a chuckle, he bid them good night, leaving Cat and Raff alone.

Apparently though, the captain's reassurance distressed Raff further. Roughly, he grabbed her about the shoulders and tipped her face into the light.

"Cat, I thought you . . . oh, never mind what I thought! What job is this you're taking? So help me, if it's some foolishness like scrubbing decks or scraping paint, I'll put you to work in the groves!"

"It's not!" She tore herself from his clutch. "What difference does it make! Oh, stop looking at me that way!"

"What way?"

"Like . . . like you despised me!"

"Is that what you think?" he exclaimed. Frustrated, Raff slapped his forehead with the heel of his hand, then he gripped the deck railing, holding it until his knuckles whitened. Visibly, his anger ebbed, and when he spoke again, his voice was controlled, matter of fact. "Regardless of your opinions, Cat, I trust you enough to let you go, and when I ask for your word, I expect you to give it. Is that clear?"

"Yes, but . . ."

His lifted brow silenced her. "I want you to promise me two things." Her nod satisfied him, and he went on. "Promise me that you'll talk to the captain as you've never talked to me. He's a man you can trust, Cat."

"Raff, I . . ."

"Promise!"

Since she'd already done as Raff asked, she gave an affirmative nod.

"That's not good enough! Tell me you will."

"I will. I promise!"

His eyes narrowed as he studied her face, then suddenly he turned away, offering her his firm, straight profile silhouetted against the flickering torchlight.

"What else, Raff?" she prompted him.

"Tell Miss Cath . . ." As he hesitated, his long tapered fingers unconsciously rubbed the bruise that had formed on his cheek. "Tell *Catherine* that I'm sorry about her aigrette. The replacement I brought was chosen before I knew she'd have no use for it. Tell her . . ."

"What makes you think I'll be seeing her again?" Cat asked, immediately regretting her outburst as Raff's contemptuous stare raked over her.

"Perhaps neither of us will," he answered coldly. Then turning on his heel, Raff strode across the deck without a good-by.

Pressing tight knuckles against her lips, Cat stifled a sob until Raff's retreating figure disappeared into the shadowy night. The sudden loss overwhelmed her— an amputation—and she hugged herself, doubling against the pain.

Whatever Raff had intended to tell her was gone now, stopped by her own foolish tongue. Gone, too, was her assurance of seeing him again. Slowly she staggered across the dock and onto the hotel grounds. Didn't he know it was heartless for him to leave her like this? Didn't he care?

He hadn't known, of course, that his leaving her as he did exposed her to Mr. Smythe's threats, and, remembering, Cat exerted caution as she crept close to the hotel building. She'd gone off without her key, expecting the door to be unlocked, but the manager had thwarted that plan, too!

Unable to leave her gowns behind with her wages, Cat had no choice but to slip in through the window. Doing so, however, was not as simple as slipping out.

150

Haste would not go well with her precarious footing on the shrub, but if she didn't hurry, the manager was apt to come searching for the singer he'd hired!

Wary of being caught, every nerve tingling, Cat tested the leafy ladder, then hoisted herself onto the sill. How glad she was for the moccasins! But as soon as she thought of them, she thought of Raff, and grief swept over her, loosening her hold. Frantically she tightened her grasp until she'd secured her position on the ledge beneath the window. Then carefully raising the panes, she slid under the glass, falling in a heap on the wooden floor. Safe!

Shaken, she closed the window and pulled the drapes, stumbling toward the lamp. The rosy glow assured her that her possessions were undisturbed, though the mirror couldn't say the same for her appearance. She'd have to do something about that and soon, she supposed, for tonight she must literally sing for her supper!

She wished she could gather her belongings and board the *Starlight* now. But, kind as the captain was, he was not a man who liked confrontations. Wanting to spare him that inconvenience, Cat had decided to wait until the time of departure before moving herself and her scant wardrobe aboard. But that meant a last performance in the hotel lounge.

Quickly she readied herself, allowing a small hope to emerge. Raff might be there! His last words had indicated otherwise; still, she felt disappointed when Lloyd Fairchild smiled at her instead.

"You're early tonight," Lloyd said as she peered beneath the archway that separated the lounge from the dining area.

"Not really. I haven't eaten yet," she said, hoping to dismiss him as she strolled past.

"Mind if I join you?" Without waiting for an answer, he hopped to her side.

"I'm afraid I'm not good company tonight, Lloyd."

He looked sheepish. "I hope it's not on my account, Miss Catherine, but I must say you've worn the sun most becomingly on those rosy cheeks." His finger touched her lightly, and she pulled away.

Until then, she'd forgotten Lloyd's juvenile groping in the boat, but the tongue lashing she'd thought to give him died unspoken. She'd no heart for arguments, and as she scanned the elaborate menu in the hotel dining hall, she realized she also had little appetite. Too bad. She would have at least liked the satisfaction of a well-eaten wage.

"Are you ill, Miss Catherine?"

"What?" She closed the menu. "No, it's been a taxing day."

"Then why not have a small steak and salad to refresh you."

"Not a salad! But, yes, a steak perhaps."

When it arrived, however, she ate only a few bites before pushing it away. Her thoughts elsewhere, she sat quietly as Lloyd chatted, and when she felt enough time had lapsed, she excused herself for the night's performance. That, too, was a disappointment. Even though she pasted on a smile, her songs lacked their usual luster, and the audience sensed the difference, responding with a mere patter of polite applause.

Afterward, she hurried to her room, hoping Lloyd would take the hint not to follow her, but his persistence proved true to form.

"Can't you see I don't want to be bothered!" she finally snapped.

"Tomorrow then?"

"Tomorrow I'll be gone!" She hadn't meant to tell him, but now that she had, she could see the news disturbed him more than she'd expected.

"I'm leaving on the *Starlight*," she explained.

"But when will I see you again?" he exclaimed, dismayed. "I can't believe you're doing this, Miss Catherine. Going off without a word!"

152

"But I just told you," she said impatiently. Then, remembering her own hurt at Raff's heartlessness, she softened her tone. "I'm sure it won't be long before the *Starlight* returns, Lloyd."

"Too long, Miss Catherine." Lightly he raised her gloved hand to his lips. "I'll be waiting for you."

Not knowing what else to say, she bid him good night, and closed the door between them, feeling emotionally drained.

In her hopes of seeing Raff again, she'd taken no time to straighten her room and a clutter of clothes awaited her. Wearily she rolled the moccasins and shirt inside Pa's overalls along with the stocking cap. No more pretenses. No more sweat-soaked hair. No more reddened hands.

When she'd placed the bundle on the washstand, she dragged herself toward the bed, too tired even to remove her dress. Sinking upon the mattress with arms outflung, her fingers brushed the package that Raff had left. What had he said? Something about a replacement for the aigrette that he'd stomped, but if these too were feathery plumes, Cat vowed to stomp them herself!

With a strangely indifferent curiosity, she raised herself onto an elbow and peeled back the paper. Beneath the plain wrap, she found, not plumes, but palmetto. A wail of anguish escaped her trembling lips as she jerked herself upright. This hat was meant for no lady! This hat was meant to cool the miserable head of a kitchen boy exactly as it'd cooled and shaded Raff's head on the river!

"Oh, no!" she cried. "He knew! He knew all along!"

CHAPTER 14

A PALE AND WEARY Catherine stepped onto the *Starlight*, her puffy eyes squinting against the newly risen sun. Behind her trailed the young hotel maid carrying her wardrobe complete with the Nile green gown. As the two swept aboard, the captain of the steamboat directed them to spacious quarters, lavishly furnished, but Cat's red-rimmed eyes were blind to the elegance.

Hesitantly, she asked the captain a favor—he'd done so much.

"If we've time, I'd appreciate saying good-by to my friends, the Tates. You've met the oldest son, Wyatt. . . ." Cautiously she looked at the maid, who was busily hanging a gown. Perhaps someday she'd have the energy to tell the girl about her escapades. Perhaps she'd even regain the humor twitching now on the captain's face.

"I recall Wyatt," he assured her. "Give the family my regards, Catherine, and I'll see you in a few hours. Now, if you'll excuse me, my dear, I've cargo to load and supplies to order yet from town."

As soon as the captain had gone, Cat dismissed the maid with a hug and her profuse thanks. Then, kicking off her pink shoes, she put on her moccasins for the walk to the Tates'. The tanned leather presented an outlandish combination with the dusky rose dress, as she hurried along the path marked by the magnolia tree, but no one was there to see.

With her own emotions in turmoil, Cat didn't notice the unusual quietness about the Tates' yard until gloomy, unscrubbed faces greeted her from the sagging porch. One look shouted that something was wrong.

"Where's Ma?" she asked, suddenly fearful.

"She's . . . she's in the bedroom," an older girl sniffed, but beyond that, no one seemed able to speak.

Cat rushed inside and tapped on the closed door before letting herself into the bedroom. The odor of illness assailed her nostrils, and her fear rose. But it wasn't Ma Tate who lay on the lumpy mattress; it was Sara Ann.

At the sound of the opening door, Ma had turned from her bedside vigil to give Cat a tired smile. Quickly, however, the older woman motioned with a plump arm for Cat to stay where she was. Not a word was spoken, but under the covers, a still form stirred.

"Mama?" The weakness of the little voice jolted Cat even more. "Is somebody here?"

"It's me, Sara Ann. Come to say hello." She took a step forward, but Ma's shaking head discouraged further movement. "If I sing you a song, will you go to sleep?" she asked, and Sara Ann stirred again. Ma nodded, and Cat began to sing—one soothing song after another until, ever so quietly, the older woman tiptoed across the room.

Cat followed her out. "What's the matter with her, Ma?"

"Darlin', I hain't shore, but I don't want you'n the others to go catchin' whatever it is."

"Has John gone for the doctor?"

Ma Tate shook her head. "He's been a-helpin' Wyatt in them groves. Sara Ann did'n' take a turn fer the worst until the night, and I did'n' wanta send the girls along in the dark, so they're a-waitin' now ta hear."

"No, Ma, I'll go. If I hurry back, I can catch a ride to town." Cat started off, then suddenly halted. "Oh, Ma! I'd come to say good-by!" she said now, realizing with dismay that she wouldn't see the family again for a while. And what if she never saw them! What if they died as Raff's family had! Rapidly, she poured out her fears to Ma and then declared, "I'll find something else to do. I'll tell the captain I can't come, and . . ."

"Hush, child! You'll do no sech thing!" Ma said as firmly as she dared without waking Sara Ann. "I'd be mighty grateful if you'd fetch that doctor for me, but then you'd best be off on the *Starlight*."

"But what if something happens, Ma!"

"Now, darlin', something always happens when the Lord's in charge, but He wants what's good and best and lovin'. He gave you a way to sing, Cat, and He'll give me and my younguns what's needed, too. Trust Him, child!"

With a sob, Cat flung herself into Ma's outstretched arms, wishing she could stay there to comfort and be comforted. Reluctantly, she tore herself away, and without looking back, she fled down the path as fast as her moccasined feet could carry her.

Despite her swiftness, Cat arrived at the dock only moments after the assigned crew had left for town, and the captain himself was nowhere to be found. In desperation, she raced to the hotel kitchen. Thankfully Archy was there.

If circumstances surrounding her plight had been less serious, the head cook's expression, when she said, "Archy, it's me, Cat," might have been funny, but she could only ignore the hanging mouth and saucer eyes as she hurriedly explained her urgent need for a ride. Precious moments passed before he took in the situation, and when he did, Archy threw down his apron and hat and fairly raced her to the door.

"I've known the Tates a mighty long time, and I shore wouldn't want nuthin' to happen to little Sara Ann."

With that thought heavy between them, they rode in silence on the small wagon that Archy had hitched to two of the hotel-owned hackneys. Thus, freed of conversation, Cat's mind raced with the clopping hooves. In a panic, however, her thoughts collided when she realized she had not a cent with which to pay a doctor.

There had to be a way! There had to be, she thought. Asking Archy's help was out of the question, but neither did Cat want Ma Tate burdened. She imagined that the woman planned to exchange fresh produce or poultry for the doctor's services, but since she had no idea how much food would be required for payment, Cat rejected the notion.

If only she hadn't bought the dress she was wearing right now, she'd have cash at hand! The fact that she hadn't needed the garment made the current predicament even more dreadful! *O Lord, if I'd only trusted You.* But she hadn't, and grieving again over the mistake was accomplishing nothing.

As she considered what to do, Cat knew it would be unfair to ask the doctor to wait for the hotel wages she'd probably never see. It could be weeks before she'd return on the *Starlight* anyway. Undoubtedly she'd receive a wage from the captain, but with other concerns predominant, she'd never thought to ask when or how much her pay would be.

What do I do, Lord? she asked silently, and

suddenly she knew. She'd have to sell her mother's locket.

As soon as the thought occurred, Cat rebelled against it, desperately searching for an alternate solution, but none appeared.

O God, do I have to? she prayerfully wondered as she clutched the treasured possession in her hand.

"Trust Him, Cat," Ma Tate had said, and with a sigh of resignation, Cat loosened her hold. She had to start somewhere, and apparently this was it.

With a word to Archy, she hopped down from the wagon in front of the bank. While the head cook sought the doctor, Cat intended to speak with Lloyd or perhaps Mr. Fairchild himself about the locket, but as she anxiously looked about the bank's cool interior, the person she most needed to speak with stepped forward.

"Miss Fairchild! You're just the person I wanted to see!"

Augusta's unexpected presence struck Cat as remarkably significant, as though God had arranged their meeting to assure Cat that she was doing what was best. A strange calm, a curious sense of peace, replaced her earlier anxiety as she unfastened the locket from around her neck and placed it in Augusta's hand.

"If you still wish to purchase the locket, it's yours."

Augusta squealed her delight. "Of course, Miss Caldwell. We must settle on a price."

Since she had no idea of the locket's actual worth, Cat trusted the offer would be sufficient to meet her need, but Augusta's suggested figure made her gasp.

"Really, Miss Caldwell, you make me wonder if my appraisal is amiss. Perhaps I've offered you too much!"

"Ten times that amount would not be worth it to me, Miss Fairchild, if sad circumstance did not

158

prevail. But since it does, I'm grateful for your generosity."

"Then we've both been pleased," Augusta said congenially. "But, truly I'm sorry for your circumstance, Miss Caldwell. I'd just assumed that Raff had changed your mind."

"Raff?" An ache pressed Cat's chest at the sound of his name.

"Yes," Augusta went on, unaware of Cat's discomfort. "Raff knew how much I admired your locket. . . . Oh, goodness! It's *my* locket now, isn't it?"

In that instant, Cat wished she could hate the beautiful young woman before her—the woman who possessed now her only prized treasure and her only love. But she couldn't. Augusta had not taken advantage of Cat's plight, and for that she was glad. Although the woman seemed somewhat frivolous and at times overbearing, Cat perceived no malice in her. Raff and the locket were in good hands.

With the transaction complete, Cat rushed to the physician's office. She paid the doctor, who assured her he was on his way. Fortunately he was familiar with the route to the Tates' house, having called upon them before when Mr. Tate's lingering illness required his services. Before departing, however, Cat obtained the doctor's promise that he would bill her if further treatment of Sara Ann or other members of the family proved necessary.

"Reckon that's all we kin do, Cat," Archy said as they left the office. Then in an attempt to cheer her flagging spirits, "Imagine me calling a lady like you 'Cat' and thinkin' you wuz a kitchen boy! If that don't beat all." With a shake of his head, Archy chuckled as he helped her onto the wagon.

"I'm glad you don't think ill of me, Archy," she said as they bounced and joggled back to the hotel. "I never meant for you to lose your kitchen help without warning."

"You wuz right good help, too, Cat—lugging that fired-up kettle across the floor." He gave another laugh. "And there I wuz, thinkin' you wuz so scrawny—fer a boy, of course. With that nice dress on, you ain't scrawny at all," he said, then suddenly looked abashed at the unwitting compliment he'd paid her trim but shapely figure.

His reddened face coaxed Cat into a smile. Laughing with him, she relayed the incidents with Mr. Smythe that had gotten her fired.

"Oh!" she exclaimed. "Archy, what if I've gotten you into trouble with the manager, too!"

"Don't 'spect I'd be as easy to fire," he grinned.

Still, Cat insisted on the assurance that all was well before returning to the *Starlight*. Reluctantly, she bid Archy farewell, telling him to give Mr. Smythe her regards after the steamboat was gone, and from the head cook's expression, she could tell he relished the scene.

"Bet that man'll drop his teeth!" Archy chuckled. "Imagine him thinkin' a lady like you'd be romancing a kitchen boy."

"Why, Archy! I don't know whether to be flattered or insulted. I just might fall in love with a kitchen boy some day!"

She sincerely doubted it however—doubted that she'd ever love anyone as much as she did Raff. If only she could be sure she'd see him again, but she wasn't. And now there was the uncertainty of ever seeing the Tates. Archy had promised to look in on them his next day off, but really there was nothing he could do—nothing Cat could do—except pray. Yet, from what Ma Tate had said, that was enough—everything.

"God is love," Ma had told her. "He kin be trusted."

Oh, she hoped so! How much she hoped so. For God, Cat was certain, was all she had.

As the *Starlight* bowed in deeper waters, Cat stood on the upper deck, squinting toward the horizon. On the banks of the hotel grounds, a few tourists waved their handkerchiefs gaily, and she responded in kind, although Archy and the maid had returned to their duties, and no familiar faces smiled back from the shore. It was just as well, she thought, turning away. A glimpse of Raff now would only deepen her despair.

Below, in her small but tastefully furnished cabin, Cat stretched out on the satin coverlet of her bed, taking in her new surroundings for the first time. A small, gray-striped satin divan reposed on one corner of the darker gray carpet that was sprinkled through-out with pink, blooming roses. A regulated stripe of tiny buds flocked the papered walls that served as a backdrop for an assortment of mahogany-framed prints, and against one wall stood a mahogany wardrobe, hand-carved with tight buds and scrolly leaves outlining the heavy double doors. Beneath a large oval wall mirror hung a three-tiered shelf, atop which stood a sterling silver candelabrum, which was, Cat realized, the only unsecured item in the room besides the heavy furniture and herself. A wise decor, she decided, though undoubtedly the *Starlight* would not pitch in a storm as would the strapped logs of a raft.

She sighed. How she wished this cruise were the beginning of her trip with Raff! How differently she'd handle the situation now. It'd been foolish, she knew, to think a man like Raff could be so easily deceived, yet she wondered that he'd said nothing, that he'd let her continue her foolishness.

He'd hinted perhaps, and looking back now, she could see his reasons for things]hich at the time made no sense. Even his violent crushing of the plumes seemed a reasonable act when she considered all that he'd confided in her about his most deeply held beliefs. Still, he had no right, unless . . . unless he thought of her as his.

His what? His friend? His child? His protected ward? But if that were so, why had he kissed her as he did? That definitely was not the sort of kiss one gave a child or a member of one's family! And he'd known. He'd known she was no stranger. He'd known her avid response as she'd returned the tantalizing pressure of his lips. And he'd known, too, that the small fist that met his cheek full-forced was hers! Yet he'd never said a word! Never said a word even while probing her discolored hand!

Wyatt Tate had told her once that Raff was a gentle man, a man who loved God. Remembering, Cat supposed that meant that he was also a man who forgave. Why, then, did she have so much trouble forgiving him for the memory of that kiss? Because he'd given it and taken it back almost in the same breath? Because she had no reason to expect another, and that in itself seemed unforgivable now.

His parting words had indicated she might never see him again, and so she'd obviously failed him in some way. But what? How? Why?

The questions riddled her, and, restless, she got up and paced about the room, struggling to let go of the darkness, the bleakness, which sang discordant notes. She willed herself to place the matter in God's hands and her own thoughts elsewhere, but doing so was no easy task. Oh, she had to get out of this room!

In her effort to escape, Cat flung open the door and fairly ran toward the encompassing sights and sounds and smells of the river. But no escape awaited her there. As she leaned against the deck railing, she felt Raff's presence everywhere. This was the river they had traveled together, the very environment they had long shared.

Each palmetto, every cypress knee, each small leaf of the gigantic live oaks reminded her of him. The

162

river, stirred by the boat's paddle, chuckled his voice, and the bright blue sky bore down like his eyes. Yet she stayed on deck until the evening breeze shivered his touch, and that reminder she could not bear. She went in, seeking the gaiety of the other passengers but found herself alone at a small round table where she carelessly took her evening meal.

Somehow she made it through her performance. The captain generously attributed her somewhat shaky presentation to first-night jitters, but when she returned to her room, annoyed with herself, she vowed that she'd never again cast shadows on stage.

"God, I need your help!"

He was there, wasn't He? Yes, Ma Tate had shown her that—shown her how to recognize the presence of a loving God in her life, and Cat felt grateful for that measure of trust, although at times, like now, it seemed so very little.

Wearily, prayerfully, she dropped onto the bed and closed her eyes. As she lay quiet, her body, mind, and spirit slowly relaxed, giving way to a hymn long forgotten that her mother had sung so many years ago.

> Jesus, Jesus, how I trust Him!
> How I've proved Him o'er and o'er!
> Jesus, Jesus, precious Jesus!
> O for grace to trust Him more!

Cat's eyes flew open, and she sat upright. That was it! That was what she needed—grace to trust. The circumstances of her life had taught her to be wary and so she'd held off God, held off Raff. No wonder he'd been hurt.

Raff had wanted her confidence in God and in herself, but also in him. And confidence meant confiding. Cat had shared her hopes, her fears, her secrets with Ma Tate, the Captain, and even Wyatt, but she'd not had the grace to trust herself fully to the man she loved.

"God is love," Ma Tate had said. "His love can be trusted." And so could Raff's, Cat knew. Perhaps their relationship as man and woman would never be complete, but she knew without a doubt that Raff wanted only what was good and loving and best for her. Raff loved her! The Lord loved her! And believing herself beloved, Cat felt that God Himself had handed her the dawn.

CHAPTER 15

THE STANDING OVATION brought tears to Cat's eyes even though by now the generous applause had become something of a routine. Whether in Jacksonville or in small towns along the way, the people responded in kind to the warmth poured out to them in song.

During these last few weeks aboard the *Starlight*, Cat had perfected her routine, adding new tunes as the lyrics came to her, but her favorite was "Dayspring", the song she'd finished at last, hoping someday Raff would hear. As she sang it now, a hush settled over the crowded lounge.

> Dark, oh dark, the sudden night has fallen.
> Bleak, oh bleak, my heart is hanging bare.
> Waiting for a glimpse of light, I'm crawlin'
> through the blackest spaces, lonely hopeless places;
> I'm waiting for love's dayspring to be there.
>> Sometimes living hurts me.
>> Sometimes no one cares.
>> Sometimes all the shadows
>> Are more than I can bear.

> Oh, please don't let's give up
> on the trust we share.
> Lighten up the spaces. Touch the lonely places.
> Hand me down the dawn, and just be there.

No one spoke. No one stirred. Then suddenly, the thundering applause shook the crystal chandeliers.

"My dear Catherine, someday you'll sink my boat with that song," the captain said as he whisked her away from the outstretched hands. How good he had been to her! And now he deposited her by her door with a grandfatherly kiss to the forehead and an admonition to rest.

Alone in her room again, Cat searched for her nightgown among the garments stuffed into her mahogany wardrobe. Not all of the clothes were hers. She'd bought new outfits for the Tates—practical outfits that they'd be inclined to wear. But word had gotten out that she preferred old-fashioned gowns for her costume, and the fabrics had flowed—velvets, satins, watered silk, beaded, seeded, pleated, and laced, some with twenty yards of cloth for skirting! How generous people had been! How kind! And the gowns had overflowed the wardrobe, into a newly acquired trunk and an assortment of boxes for hats—none of which, she was glad to say, were furred or feathered.

With scant room for everyday clothes, she'd purchased only a dress or two with matching accessories—including, of course, a parasol. It amazed her still that she had a purseful of cash, not only from her wages but from gratuities given by her appreciative audience. She'd refused such gifts, but they'd come anyway, along with dozens of roses and scores of proposals, none of which she'd taken seriously. Yet the attention had buoyed her spirits when at her lowest ebb, and she praised God for the love she'd received, the love she'd been shown.

But where was that nightgown? she wondered,

knowing full well she'd never sleep. Tonight was the last stop on the St. John's. Tomorrow they'd dock at Siloam Springs.

She wondered if Raff would be impressed if he learned she could bicycle. Rather precariously, she'd balanced for the first time on the two-wheeler when a cycling club in Jacksonville had requested her entertainment for one of their weekly meetings. She'd been so enamored with the sport and the ideal transportation, which required no feeding, that she'd purchased a two-wheeler of her own. Oh, wouldn't Sara Ann be surprised on the morrow when Cat rolled onto the Tates' yard!

The wings of her brow touched as the elusive "what if's" flitted through her mind, but with an impatient flick of her hand, Cat banished the morbid thought. Whatever happened, God was in charge: He could be trusted; Love could be trusted. And in her chemise instead of a nightgown, surprisingly, Cat slept.

She awoke with the sun, and after an hour or two of wearing down the wooden planks on the deck, the captain steered her into the dining room where he presumed to order buttermilk to calm her cocoon of a stomach. Obediently, she sipped, nibbling bites of water crackers in between.

"And to whom do you attribute this sudden state of nerves, my dear?" the captain asked in gentle jest. "Surely your Mr. Jordan weighs too heavily on your mind."

"Hmmm. Jordan. That name does have a familiar tone," she answered him.

"Yes, as I recall you were traveling companions many moons ago," the captain went on, lightly teasing.

But suddenly Cat grew serious. "Not too many moons, I hope. Oh, captain! So much has happened to me these last few weeks, what if Raff . . . Now there! I promised myself I wouldn't worry."

Reaching across the clothed table, the captain patted her hand. "Ah, Catherine. Still that defenseless little girl at heart. Yet I marvel at how you've blossomed aboard my ship."

"Have I?" A flush of pleasure crept above the lace around her throat. She hoped Raff would think so too, but perhaps it was too late; perhaps it didn't matter.

"You should be glad, my dear, not frowning. Catherine . . ." The captain toyed with his water goblet. "Catherine, a steamboat is no home for a girl like you—at least, not a permanent home," he amended.

"But you just said . . ."

"I know, my dear. You've blossomed here, and I mean every word of that. You know you're welcome here, too, and when you leave, I shall long miserably for your refreshing company. But, Catherine, if a time should come for you to go, I trust you'll know, and I'll require no explanations."

Lovingly she pressed his hand against her cheek and thanked him. Then teasing once again, she said, "Oh, good! You'll not fire me."

"Never, my dear. Never."

Their conversation relieved Cat immensely, for she'd grown to care deeply about the captain. She was well aware that her astounding popularity had increased the *Starlight*'s clientele, which previously had been on the decline. Tourist trade remained about the same, but residents of their river stops had filled the lounge and dining hall nightly when word got around, "Catherine Caldwell is singing!" What a joy it had been—and a responsibility to those she sought to entertain—and Cat had flourished under the loving attention of her audiences.

Still, it had been lonely. At first, that amazed her—that so much honor, so many people, so much attention could make less difference than the simple caring of a single friend. The captain's interest in her,

168

his kindness, filled more space than thousands could, but still—he wasn't Raff.

Her heartbeat quickened as she stepped onto the deck again, knowing that in the next hours she'd see him, for she'd decided that if he did not come to her, she would indeed find him. She'd no doubts now that, unless his relationship with Augusta Fairchild had changed, he'd be happy to see her. Or unless someone else had come onto the scene. The maybe's worried her when she allowed them to, but she knew now that a spark, a zest, an enthusiastic interest existed between a man and a woman who were in love. She'd observed the phenomenon often upon the *Starlight*, from newlyweds to those who enjoyed the mellow glow of mature love. And that special look did not exist between Augusta and Raff. She'd seen it, though. She'd seen it in his incredibly blue eyes. And the look had been for her alone.

A shiver of excitement gained momentum as Cat caught sight of the hotel at Siloam Springs, and she could barely keep from hopping about like a child. Impatiently she squinted at the faces of onlookers who slowly gathered on the shore, but Raff's was not among them. She sighed. More waiting, but not idly so.

While the steamboat docked, Cat gathered the items she'd purchased for the Tates, and changed into the Turkish trousers and short, double-breasted jacket of her bicycle dress, a gray and white serge trimmed with bright yellow piping. Her hair was pinned lightly in a knot atop her head. Then she buttoned her close-fitting boots of soft black kid. Ready!

By now, the passengers aboard had gone off to meet relatives or visit the Springs, so Cat enlisted the aid of one of the crew who could spare a few moments to obtain her two-wheeler from the cargo hold. She pushed it herself across the dock then pedaled across the grounds to the kitchen house. Archy, however, was not around.

Since she'd had no word on the Tates, Cat had hoped to prepare herself, for good or ill, with a quick report from the head cook. But the arrival of the *Starlight* had coincided with Archy's afternoon reprieve from the kitchen. She pedaled to the magnolia-marked path, steering clear of Mr. Smythe's office and the main building of the hotel.

The bicycle sped her journey, except for the occasional foot-push required to wheel over a fallen limb or weedy clump. Despite her novice skill at balancing and her small, sacked burden of clothes, Cat cycled into view of the rust-stained roof in almost half her normal traveling time. She felt pleased with herself and with that pleasure and the warming sun, her complexion fairly glowed. But when she heard the everyday sounds of chicks and children, her face broke into a grin. All was well!

In the yard, the older girls called Ma when they saw Cat coming, and threw down the basket of clothes that they'd been collecting from the line. Cat left them exclaiming over her two-wheeler as she rushed toward Ma. Sitting on the porch swing, Sara Ann shouted but stayed put as Cat gave Ma Tate a hug.

"Well, Sara Ann, don't I get a hug from you?" she teased, but something in Ma's face cautioned her. An awkward silence stretched minutes out of an actual second or two before Cat bounded onto the porch, scooping the child into her arms.

"Oh, my, you look so fine, Sara Ann!" And the little girl did, too, except for the limbs lying limp on the slatted seat.

"Them legs don't work too good," Sara Ann stated matter-of-factly. "Have you brung me a new song, Cat?" she asked with a bounce from her upper body.

Cat bit her lip. If Sara Ann could accept her condition, so would she. "I brought you enough songs

170

to sing from now 'til Christmas. And . . ." She rummaged through her sack. "I've brought you a brand-new dress."

"Oh! Oh! Oh!" was all the wide-eyed little girl could say.

Flocking to the porch to see, the other girls giggled their delight when Cat whisked out dresses for them, too. For Ma, however, she'd purchased an embroidered shawl, and for Wyatt and John, a lightweight shirt each.

"Child, wha' did you go a-spendin' all your hard-earned money fer?" Ma scolded, though the shawl had obviously pleased her.

"I didn't, Ma! People gave me more than I could spend on myself."

"To hear you sing?"

Cat nodded with a grin. "God's gifts just keep on giving, don't they, Ma? And now I've had the fun of buying you each a birthday present."

"It hain't nobody's birfday," Sara Ann insisted.

Cat laughed at the little girl's outrage. "But think of all the birthdays I've missed with you, Sara Ann!" And at that, the child giggled, hugging her new dress tightly.

"Where's John?" Cat asked, looking around.

Ma hesitated. "He's stayin' out at Raff's fer a while, Cat. His legs is fine, but his arms pert near caused him grief. Raff sed he'd see to it John worked them muscles back, so Wyatt's been a-helpin' me." Her eyes darted to Sara Ann, and Cat understood. Although still young, the child was almost as large as Cat herself, and lifting her often would be too taxing for Ma Tate or the girls.

"What was it, Ma?" she whispered, but Sara Ann heard and answered.

"Me'n John got took with polio, Cat, and it wuz awful!" Then with the elasticity of childhood, she added, "Kin I try on my new dress, Ma? Please?"

171

As soon as Ma had consented, the older girls formed a "chair" with their arms and hoisted Sara Ann off the swing and into the house. Cat waited until they were out of earshot before asking about the doctor's prognosis.

"Time and the Lord'll tell," Ma stated. "Only thing I kin do is pray and work them muscles when I kin."

But Ma looked tired, and Cat imagined the strain of exercising Sara Ann's legs had taken its toll.

"If only there were some way she could exercise herself," Cat started, but Ma shook her head.

"I've prayed and prayed, Cat, but I cain't think of nuthin'."

Immediately, however, Cat did.

"My bicycle! Sara Ann is not that much smaller than I am, Ma! It's perfect!"

But Ma Tate wasn't so sure.

"Don't you see, Ma! I thought I was buying the two-wheeler for myself, for transportation, especially to come see you! But I wasn't!"

The older woman looked skeptical. "Now, Cat, don't you go a-tellin' me fibs."

"Ma, just because I didn't know why that bicycle was needed doesn't mean that the Lord wasn't at work. He was! And it's the answer to your prayers!"

"Well, I never!" she replied, and then her face crumpled in grateful relief.

Each of the girls had a wobbly, gleeful turn on the bicycle, wearing old dresses, of course. Sara Ann's independent success proved small, but with someone on either side, and a third person helping her feet stay on the pedals, she beamed at Ma and Cat. The two women, however, felt disheartened when they saw how much help would still be required in exercising, and it wasn't until Wyatt returned home from the field with the idea of strapping her feet to the pedals and building a stationary stand that the whole idea seemed, at last, workable.

Yet neither the bicycle nor Sara Ann upon it caught Wyatt's first attention when he sauntered into the yard. It was Cat. She saw him coming and rushed out to meet him, but his look of total confoundment slowed her pace. No one had told him!

"Wyatt," Cat called his name softly, then walked toward him, holding out her hand. "It's me. Cat."

"I cain't believe hit!" he exclaimed when he'd found his voice, and his eyes were two full moons. "That's yore face fer shore, Cat, but . . ." His complexion traveled through several shades of sunburn.

"It's me," she said again. "How've you been?"

He looked at his feet. "Reckon I cain't complain—though that's about all Raff's done since you've been gone. Guess now I see why." His boot scuffed carelessly in the sand.

"He didn't tell you anything?" Nor Ma, nor John, nor the girls? She couldn't believe it! How many loyal friends had kept her secrets?

"'Spect I'm 'bout the slowest creature you ever seen."

"Oh, no, Wyatt! It wasn't like that at all. I'm the one who was slow to catch on—slow to trust. I . . . I didn't have anything to wear but my father's clothes, and even if I had. . . ."

"That would've been plumb foolish! A girl, travelin' alone." He looked her in the eyes now, brightening.

"You forgive me then?" she asked somewhat shyly.

"'Course!"

"Think Raff will?"

Shaking his head, Wyatt shrugged. "Raff's been a-actin' real strange, Cat, ever since he tol' me you'd gone off on that steamboat. Don' eat nuthin' and is sheer grumpiness hitself." He looked at her sharply. "'Tain't funny, Cat!"

173

"You're right, Wyatt," she said, suppressing a giggle. "But it makes me happy just the same."

Ma invited Cat to stay for supper, and, for that matter, as long as she liked, but well before dusk, Cat felt an urgency to return to the *Starlight*. Since Ma and the girls had chores to attend to and Wyatt had begun nailing together the frame for "Sara Ann's contraption", Cat skipped down the path alone. What a perfectly splendid day!

She hoped it would remain so into the evening. Although she had no knowledge of Raff's plans, something told her she'd see him tonight. Just thinking about it made her tremble! She wondered if he were still angry with her, still hurt that she'd shown so little trust. What would he say? What would *she* say? What would she *wear!*

The words, she prayed, would come, but her attire demanded careful planning on her part. Alone again in her cabin, she studied her wardrobe critically. If Raff came for the evening's performance, she wanted to be wearing her favorite costume, the brown velvet gown that she herself had stitched to fit after the hotel maid's expert pinning. She'd since purchased elbow-length gloves of a creamy yellow color that matched the full-blown roses that splashed against one panel of the skirt, the blooms stopping just short of the gown's long train. A rose also capped one sleeveless shoulder at the top edge of the low scooped bodice—not too low though—covered with brown lace. The lace accentuated her gentle curves and called attention to a graceful neck. How beautiful the locket would have looked around her throat! But a velvet ribbon of creamy yellow had sufficed.

Since it was too early to don the brown velvet gown, Cat slipped on the pale gray faille she'd succumbed to in a small shop in Jacksonville. The faddish color, however, was brightened immensely by the embroidered cherry velvet that collared the scoop

174

neck. Ballooned sleeves hit above the elbow, requiring gloves, and Cat sincerely hoped she was not overdressed. How much she wanted to look her best for Raff! And this was the only gown he'd yet to see of her everyday attire. She supposed she should have purchased a blue serge suit or a simple cotton frock, but it was too late now!

Nervously she repinned her hair in place, leaving a wisp of curl to fringe her neck and forehead. Then she strolled onto the lower deck, milling about with the passengers who'd returned for the evening meal.

She wondered if she'd have to eat alone. Often she did when the captain was busy, as he seemed to be today. At first she hadn't minded since she'd had such fun selecting anything she'd wanted from the menu. Eventually she'd sampled everything—the terrapin, the broiled trout in anchovy sauce, the smoked beef tongue—for which passengers had to pay twenty-five to forty cents! How fortunate she felt to have her meals included. Yet room and board had its drawbacks. The asparagus she'd grown to love cost two whole dimes while other vegetables were half that amount. She'd felt guilty about its cost until she reminded herself that she seldom took the macaroons or meringue pie offered for dessert.

When Raff didn't come, Cat wandered toward the dining room, thinking it just as well. She needed nourishment to sustain her throughout the evening performance, but if Raff were at table with her, she'd be too unnerved to eat! As she ventured in that direction, however, a familiar voice called her name. Cat sighed. It was Lloyd.

Placing a smile on her disappointed face, she turned to greet him. The wind had ruffled his blond hair, but he looked quite dashing in his fitted waistcoat and slim trousers of pin-striped gray. His handsome face glowed at the sight of her, and her echoed name became an exclamation.

"Catherine! You look marvelous!"

She gave a slight curtsy, thanking him, but her eyes rested on his. Although Lloyd appeared pleased and delighted with her lovely presence, no special spark shone, and Cat breathed her relief. Regardless of the outcome with Raff, she'd dreaded facing Lloyd, facing the love in his eyes, before turning him away.

Instead, she took his arm, glad for the company, as she accepted his invitation to dine. Seated amidst the clatter of sterling and the tinkle of crystal, they agreed on tame duck with applesauce and fried oyster plant to accompany the favored asparagus.

As soon as the order was placed, Lloyd said once again, "You really do look marvelous, Catherine." But then he fell unusually quiet, staring at her until their plates, emptied, had been cleared away.

Cat expected to excuse herself, but Lloyd reached for her hand, clasping it tightly.

"Marry me, Catherine."

"What!" He'd caught her so totally unaware with his proposal that Cat jerked her hand away as she exclaimed, knocking a goblet to the floor. It shattered.

Lloyd grimaced. "Why do I have the feeling that that was my heart, breaking into a million pieces?"

"Oh, don't be so dramatic, Lloyd!" she snapped. Then she added, more softly, "I'm sorry, but you don't love me, Lloyd, even though you may think you do."

"But I do, Miss Catherine!"

"Well, I don't love you," she said bluntly. "I'm sorry," she apologized once again, seeing his stricken face, "but I never meant to . . . to lead you on. I thought we were . . . friends, Lloyd. Nothing more." She hated being so abrupt, but Lloyd seemed to understand little else.

A blond eyebrow lifted. "You've met someone else, haven't you? I knew it! I knew if I let you go, this would happen!"

"You're partly right," Cat admitted. "I do love someone else, Lloyd, but I knew him before the *Starlight* sailed."

Astonishment swept his handsome face. "But . . . but . . . I've never seen you with anyone else except Raff, and . . ." Her downcast eyes told everything. "My word, Catherine! Are you in love with that infantile fool, Raff Jordan?"

"How dare you call him that!"

"Then it's true! Answer me, Catherine. I've just offered you a proposal of marriage. You owe me the truth!"

"All right! Yes! Yes! Are you satisfied now?"

The blond head shook. "No, but I suppose that doesn't matter, does it?"

How often had she told herself that! It didn't matter? But hearing it from Lloyd, her sympathies fled, for him and for herself. He preferred his pity self-contained.

She rose, stepping with lifted skirts as the steward swept aside the remaining bits of glass.

"Be happy, Lloyd. I'd have made you a terrible wife," she gently soothed. "Will you stay for my performance?"

"Why should I?" he sulked.

"Because I like you, and you like me. Because we're friends. Because I can't give you my heart, but I can give you a song or two."

Suddenly he grinned up at her. "Who's being dramatic now?" he teased, and she laughed. Then with a deep curtsy generally reserved for the finale of her musical performance, Cat excused herself, leaving Lloyd behind with a half-accepting smile.

As she completed her toilette an hour or so later, Cat patted her hair with nervous fingers. Perhaps she'd been mistaken. Perhaps Raff wouldn't come. She smoothed the nap on the brown velvet gown and adjusted her yellow neck ribbon with a critical scowl. Perhaps she'd overdone her attire.

The effect was pleasing, she admitted, as she cocked her head in front of the oval glass. The velvety brown was almost the same shade as her hair, though she hoped Raff would notice more than that! If, of course, he came. . . .

A tap on the door startled her as the captain came to escort her to the lounge.

"We've a full house tonight, my dear, and you wouldn't have to sing a note, looking as beautiful as you do."

"Did you . . . did you see Raff?" she had to ask.

"No," he admitted slowly, "but, Catherine . . ." The sentence died on set lips.

"What?"

"Nothing, my dear. I'm a silly old man who's afraid of seeing you disappointed."

Cat inhaled a steadying breath. So. He hadn't come. Her chin lifted, lengthening her creamy throat, and her shoulders straightened in their velvety caps. In the lounge, dozens of other people *had* come—come to hear her sing, come to be entertained—and she'd not allow her disappointment to shadow their evening.

"Ready?" the captain asked with a sad, sweet smile.

"Ready."

The applause began even before her kidskin slippers touched the carpet in the lounge, and the sound evoked a truer smile as Cat swept in. Her green eyes darted around the luxurious room, broadening her smile as she recognized several faces. Lloyd had remained after all, and she blew him a kiss, returning his. Everyone sobered and quieted, waiting.

She borrowed a song from Johanna Maria, better known as the late Jenny Lind, but most of the numbers she selected were of her own making.

178

Ballads, love songs, nameless tunes, lively or sad, rang out, with varied tempo and each building to a crescendo of clapping hands. Undoubtedly the concert was a success. She'd entertained, and for a moment, she'd forgotten Raff, forgotten herself.

Having reached her final number, Cat hesitated. "Dayspring" was the song she'd wanted so to share with Raff, and tonight she couldn't bear to sing it except to him. She'd have to select another number, and alert the pianist to the change in schedule, she thought as she scanned the faces of the waiting audience.

But there was no need. Leaning against the entrance of the crowded room, his tall form caused her pulse to gallop with such speed she had to look away simply to begin.

Dark, oh, dark,
The sudden night has fallen . . .
Bleak, oh, bleak,
My heart is hanging bare . . .

It was a song to which the audience responded. It was a song that expressed their loneliness, their hurts, their despair, but as she sang the last lines, Cat directed the words to Raff.

Oh, please don't let's give up on the trust we share . . .
Lighten up the spaces . . .
Touch the lonely places . . .
Hand me down the dawn,
And just be there.

But he was lost in the crowd.

Applause and snatching hands held her back until the captain came to her rescue, clearing a path and whispering, "You might try the top deck, my dear."

She did. Racing up the stairs in the dark, Cat glimpsed his pale blue jacket as a movement near the railing caught the torchlight. Although her slippered feet made no sound, he seemed to sense her presence,

179

and he turned, those incredibly blue eyes fastening quickly upon her.

If she'd thought to throw her arms around him, his stance forbade it. His own arms folded across his chest. She stopped. Hesitantly she swayed toward him in a billow of petticoats that she'd acquired to round her bustled skirt.

"You're looking well," he said.

His low voice caused a tremor. "And so do you."

"Traveling suits you."

"Not as well as staying where I'm wanted."

"Cat . . ."

"Raff . . ."

She giggled as both spoke at once. But neither had their turn.

Lloyd's voice cut through their expectancy as he strode across the deck to Cat's side. "I thought I might find you here." He gave Raff a spiteful glance before ignoring him completely. "Catherine, I know what you said, but I can't let you go. Would it help if I got on my knees?"

"You'd only muss your trousers," she scolded.

"But, Catherine, you hardly know this man. No offense, Raff, but . . ."

"That's enough, Lloyd!" Cat broke in sharply. "I know this man quite well, thank you. I should. I traveled with him for *weeks* on the river," she added, mischievously emphasizing the duration of time spent on the raft.

"You what?" Lloyd exclaimed. "I don't believe it!" He looked to Raff unwillingly for confirmation, and, at his nod, gave a cry of alarm.

"See, Lloyd? I told you I'd make a terrible wife."

"Ooooh, Catherine," the poor man moaned his discontent. Speechless after that utterance, he descended the stairs in haste.

"I suppose I've just ruined my reputation," Cat said, but her lips twitched.

Raff, however, was not amused. In one long stride, he reached her, and placing the flat of his hand against her back, he steered her rather roughly to an uninhabited corner, away from the passengers who had just stepped onto the deck. Seizing her by the shoulders, he turned her toward him.

"Did Lloyd ask you to marry him?" Raff demanded.

"Yes, but I refused."

"So I gathered," he said dryly. "And here I thought you two were relative strangers!"

Strangers? The word hit a note.

"Why, Raff Jordan! You were spying on me! You saw Lloyd mauling me in that rowboat on the Springs.

"I wasn't spying! I was merely trying to find you."

"Perhaps," she said softly, "I was waiting to be found."

His hands slid down her gloved arms, and she arched toward him, wanting the gentle joy, the fiery passion of his kiss, but instead he gripped her elbows!

"Cat, what did Lloyd mean? About me? About us?"

Averting her eyes, she gave a little shrug. "Something I said, I guess."

"What?" A knuckle relentlessly tilted her heart-shaped face toward him.

"I . . . I told him I didn't love him. I told him I'm in love with you."

"You told him *what?*" His disgust alarmed her. "But why, Cat? Why didn't you tell *me?*"

"I just did!" she snapped. "And, if you were listening, I told you tonight in my song. I would have told you before—long before—but I was afraid . . . afraid you didn't want me."

"Oh, Kitten." His breath warmed the top of her head as he held her as close as the layers of petticoat would allow. "I'm sorry."

She tensed. "For what?"

"For not letting you know I was waiting." He laughed. "The first time I laid eyes on you, I knew you were one special little lady."

She gasped. "That soon!"

He nodded. "But I thought you needed time to find that out for yourself." His low voice sounded husky. "I love you, Cat. Have I waited too long to tell you?"

"Oh, Raff!" she exclaimed before answering him with a kiss.

Tenderly at first, his lips brushed hers, then, caressing, exploring, his kiss thundered through her like wave after wave of applause. When he finally broke away, she leaned against his heaving chest, thinking no encore could be so exhilarating. But she was wrong The next kiss left her trembling.

"Kitten," he murmured against her silken cheek, "we're attracting an audience."

"Hmmm." She snuggled deeper against him. "Do you mind?"

"Not for myself, but then your reputation is already ruined, isn't it?" He laughed. "I wouldn't have missed Lloyd's face for the world. You'll have to marry me, I guess."

Yanking herself free, Cat glowered at him. "Raff Jordan, that's the worst proposal I've ever had!"

"Oh? And how many proposals have you received thus far, Miss Caldwell?"

"Dozens! Oh, don't look so shocked." She stamped her foot. "I did nothing to encourage a single one!"

"All right! All right!" He took her hand and lifted it to his lips with a low bow. "Miss Caldwell, I humbly ask for this hand in marriage—assuming, of course, that it's neither red nor purple nor . . ."

She jerked her hand away and placed it on one hip. "Raff, what am I supposed to tell our children? That you refused to be serious even in proposing?"

"Ah!" One eyebrow lifted jauntily. "Now that we

have children, Mrs. Jordan, I suggest we marry immediately."

"Oh, Raff." She couldn't help giggling until his lips reminded her he was very serious indeed.

"Wait," he said at last, "you're making me forget."

"What?" She'd kept her arms around his neck, but now he loosened her hold.

"I don't want you to get the idea that you wangled a marriage contract out of me by scandalizing Lloyd." He reached into his pocket, but whatever he drew out was tightly concealed in his hand. "We'll choose a ring tomorrow, Cat, if you've no objections."

"None."

"I would have done so before, but I wasn't sure what size to get, nor whether you preferred an emerald or a diamond."

"Both," she teased.

"However," he continued, undaunted, "I hope you'll accept this as a seal of our betrothal and a sign of my love."

"What is it?" she squealed when he made her close her eyes. But she knew, and her breath held the dawning of that priceless moment.

Behind her, Raff dropped a tender kiss on the nape of her neck. "I love you, Cat," he said. And then he fastened into its rightful place her mother's locket.

ABOUT THE AUTHOR

MARY HARWELL SAYLER is a writer on the move! With her Seattle-born husband, she has lived in many states and attended a variety of churches of all denominations, broadening her appreciation and understanding of people and places. Her three children were born in Southern states, and the Sayler family now resides in Deland, Florida.

Mary is a prolific writer and holds membership in the Society of Children's Book Writers, the Florida Freelance Writer's Association, and the Christian Writers Fellowship, for which she serves as a writing instructor.

A Letter To Our Readers

Dear Reader:

Pioneering is an exhilarating experience, filled with opportunities for exploring new frontiers. The Zondervan Corporation is proud to be the first major publisher to launch a series of inspirational romances designed to inspire and uplift as well as to provide wholesome entertainment. In order that we might better contribute to your reading enjoyment, we would appreciate your taking a few minutes to respond to the following questions and return to:

> Anne Severance
> Zondervan Publishing House
> 1415 Lake Drive, S.E.
> Grand Rapids, Michigan 49506

1. Did you enjoy reading HAND ME DOWN THE DAWN?
   - ☐ Very much. I would like to see more books by this author!
   - ☐ Moderately
   - ☐ I would have enjoyed it more if _____

2. Where did you purchase this book? _____

3. What influenced your decision to purchase this book?
   - ☐ Cover
   - ☐ Title
   - ☐ Publicity
   - ☐ Back cover copy
   - ☐ Friends
   - ☐ Other _____

4. Please rate the following elements from 1 (poor) to 10 (superior):

☐ Heroine   ☐ Plot
☐ Hero   ☐ Inspirational theme
☐ Setting   ☐ Secondary characters

5. Which settings would you like to see in future Serenade/Saga Books?

_____   _____

_____   _____

6. What are some inspirational themes you would like to see treated in future Serenade books?

_____   _____

_____   _____

7. Would you be interested in reading other Serenade/Saga or Serenade/Serenata Books?

☐ Very interested
☐ Moderately interested
☐ Not interested

8. Please indicate your age range:

☐ Under 18   ☐ 25–34   ☐ 46–55
☐ 18–24   ☐ 35–45   ☐ Over 55

9. Would you be interested in a Serenade book club? If so, please give us your name and address:

Name _____

Occupation _____

Address _____

City _____ State _____ Zip _____

Serenade/Saga Books are inspirational romances in historical settings, designed to bring you a joyful, heart-lifting reading experience.

Serenade/Saga books now available in your local bookstore:

Watch for these Serenade Books in the coming months: